CRUEL WAR

DANI RENÉ

From *USA Today* Bestselling Author Dani René comes a new adult romance filled with lies, secrets, and steam!

I hate her. I want Dahlia to pay. Tynewood is my town, and she doesn't belong here. While rage fuels me, my blood burns with desire.
I want vengeance, and I'll get it.
No. Matter. What.
We're on opposite sides of the battlefield — a poised flower, a raging warrior, and a mountain of secrets between us.

I knew he was bad news the moment I laid eyes on him. Anger and lust swirl together when he looks at me, but I don't know why. War has commenced, and as secrets unfold, it looks like the battle has only just begun.
He wants to hurt me. He loves to see me cry. What Ares Lancaster doesn't realize is, I'm not afraid of the darkness inside him.

Lies. Revenge. Bloodshed.
When war comes to a head, nobody is safe from the destruction it leaves in its wake.

Revenge, like power and greed, is insatiable.
It craves, it poisons, and it infests you like an
addiction, and you'll never be free.

WELCOME TO

History has a way of repeating itself.

Long ago, the world was ravaged by men who believed they were gods. They knew that with wealth would come supremacy and the possibility to reign, creating a society with limitless power.

A chosen handful of self-proclaimed rulers, who wanted more, took it upon themselves to band together.

Hungry for the privilege and influence that came with being one of the men who would sit at the table within the society aptly named, the Gilded Sovereign.

The men, who became known as the Crowns, would be succeeded by their firstborn sons on their twenty-first birthday, walking the halls of Tynewood University as if they're paved in gold.

Whispered about by mere mortals.

The Sovereign reveled in the domination afforded to them.

They wanted people to bow down to them. To fear them. They believed that when fear was present, respect would inadvertently come with it.

With every year that passed and each new generation claimed their seat at the table, the darkness took over. When mortals hold the future in their hands the way the Sovereign do, only bad things can happen.

Men hunger for more. They crave it like an addict hungers for his next fix. But they didn't realize that the one thing that gifted them the power could also bring them to their knees.

All their secrets are kept locked up tight.

They not only rule their town but the country. There is one rule they vow to hold till death—never speak of the society drenched in money and power.

War. Love. Life. Death.

Wealthy. Stylish. Powerful. Regal.

Deviant. Destructive. Dangerous. Deadly.

By blood. By oath.

Four young men will take charge as their fathers step down. They'll be the future leaders—heartless and cold. Nothing can change their fate, and nobody can stop their path. This is their destiny.

The town of Tynewood is their playground. A place where the rich and famous come to hide their most depraved acts within the small, almost forgotten town.

Darkness lurks within the walls of Tynewood University, and danger simmers just beneath the surface. If you look closely, you'll see the depravity that reigns supreme.

Welcome to the inner sanctum.

A society of gods.

Welcome to the Gilded Sovereign.

PROLOGUE

I'M PACING A PATHWAY IN THE CARPET OF MY office as I think about the future. My youngest son's sixteenth birthday is coming up, and I know I'm going to have to tell him about the Sovereign. But I have a feeling he already knows.

Glancing at the clock on the wall above the fireplace, I note it's almost midnight. My plan is in place for next week. It took me years to make sure I had the right people in my corner. And it's finally time.

My office door clicks open, and Philipe saunters in with a smile on his face. My eldest son, who is eighteen now, is like me: cold and ruthless, and he doesn't care for anyone outside our family. That's what a true Sovereign is, but

1

Ares, I worry about him. I don't know if he has it in him to join us.

"The job is done," Philipe tells me, satisfaction on his face at the admission. The blood splattered on his shirt is evidence that he's finished the job correctly.

"Good," I nod, before turning to my desk to pick up the folder. Philipe will take over the head of the table from me when he turns twenty-one, but he's been doing odd jobs for me since he came of age.

Once he joins the Sovereign, he'll have all the power I ensured for him. This is our legacy. I hand him the manila folder and watch him flip it open.

"They voted this evening," I tell him. "You're taking my seat at the table, you'll only be sworn in when you hit the age set out in our history. Ares will be the second chair once he's old enough."

"I doubt Greg will be happy about this," my son remarks. The second eldest member of the Crowns, Gregory Birchwood, wasn't happy about two Lancasters at the table, but he can't do anything about it. His daughter isn't allowed to step up. Grecia Birchwood isn't meant to wear the gilded crown.

"He made his vote. There's no going back. The oath was signed; blood was shed." I make my way to the armoire, which sits in the corner of my office and pour myself and Philipe a shot of whiskey. Handing a tumbler to him, I lift my own. "To the Sovereign and the rule of the Lancasters." I clink my glass on my son's, and a smile beams from his face.

It's uncanny how much he looks just like his mother. There's a soft golden hue to his light brown hair, and his eyes, the color of the freshly grown grass on a hot summer's day, match hers almost identically. I watch him take a sip before he narrows his gaze on me.

"I'm leaving," he utters. "I'm ready to go to New York. It's the one thing I've wanted, and it's time. I'll be back for my inking."

"I didn't think you'd stay, but remember, if we need you…" I allow my words to trail into the heavy silence in the office. He doesn't realize what being an Elder means, but he'll learn.

We still have time before Ares, Etienne Durand, and Tarian Calvert come of age, so Philipe will take the reins until the three younger boys step up and they form one entity.

Philipe swallows down the amber liquid before offering me a grin. "I'll be here whenever you need me."

"Go, I know you're itching to get to your girl," I tell him, shaking my head when he chuckles.

"See you tomorrow." He leaves me in the office with my thoughts. I've done things in my life that were needed to ensure my family are safe. Even though most wouldn't agree with my actions, it is my choice, and I'll never apologize.

My phone rings shrilly on the desk; when I pick it up, I note the name before answering. "What?"

"We found her. She's a crown," he tells me. I knew they would. The men I have around the country, around the world, would've tracked her down one way or another, and she knows it.

"Good, we'll keep an eye on her. The father?"

"He's around."

"Bring him in, the job I have for him is important. I want it done next week." Hanging up, I smile when I pour myself another drink and savor the burn of the whiskey as it travels down my throat.

I sit back and stare out the window. The full moon is high, reminding me of how small and insignificant we truly are in the grand scheme of things. But I also know that nothing can stop the events that will take place in the coming years.

My sons will rule the Sovereign with iron fists.

I gulp down the last of my drink as my office door opens, and my wife strolls in. She's my life. I fell for her when I was a boy, and even though she knows of the darkness that resides inside me, she hasn't run; she continues to love me even after all the shit I've put her through.

"Are you coming to bed?"

"I am. Philipe was just here to collect a docket," I tell her, crooking my finger to call her closer. "Ares will know about his new role in this household. I plan to speak to him tomorrow."

"I don't know if he's ready," she shakes her head, worry etched on her beautiful face. She voices my concerns out loud.

Sighing, I stand and go to where she's standing at the edge of my desk, pulling her into my arms. "He will be. He's a Lancaster, it's in our blood."

"This isn't some supernatural occurrence, Abner. He's not going to suddenly become powerful and grow wings," she bites out in frustration. Our son may not be something from a comic book, but there are things about the four new Crowns who will take over that nobody would ever guess.

Ares being one of them.

But what she doesn't know can't hurt her, which is why I'm not the one to complete the task I've set in motion. So instead of saying anything, I scoop her up and make my way through the house and up to our suite.

"I think it's time we made love again," I murmur in her ear, with my eyes shut, I pray she'll calm the fuck down. The darkness grips me when I think of the violence to befall us.

Her hands land on my shoulders, holding me away from her for a moment before she shakes her head. "Don't push me away and treat me like I'm fragile."

"You are fragile." I can easily overpower her, and she knows it. I could lift her with one hand, squeeze, and her breath will be stolen. I don't. I do allow her to glower at me though because that will ensure our night in bed together will be short.

"I'm not, Abner," she bites out, and I can see this night isn't going as planned. All I need, want, was a chance to feel her, but she's not having it.

I rise, turning away from her, and head into the bathroom. I don't need this. I really can't lose my shit so close to Philipe's inking.

The moment my eldest son wears the mark of the Sovereign, I can take a back seat on the day to day running of the society.

"Don't walk away from me," she retorts, her voice shrill and angry.

"Darling, I suggest you go to bed."

"Like fuck, this is ridiculous. What are you not telling me? You've hidden enough from me over the years, Abner. The women, the killing, I see the blood on your clothes; I'm not stupid."

One rule of the Sovereign is to never speak of it with those outside the society. Even our partners. The only people who know about it are the children who will step up to the table.

No females.

No outsiders.

It may sound misogynistic, but that's what the ancestors wanted, and that's what they'll get. We observe their rituals, their way of life.

"Abner."

"Lilian. Go. To. Bed." My voice is low, a warning tone that makes her stop for a moment. I feel her. Every part of me knows what she feels because I can feel it, too. I sense every argument she has raging around in her mind.

I glance over my shoulder, meeting her questioning gaze before she shakes her head and turns away from me. I watch her slip under the sheet and curl into a ball. Her shoulders shake, but I don't go to her. I'm not that type of man.

Closing my eyes, I quell the urges inside me, and I calm my erratic heartbeat. My sons don't know about me; they have no idea who their father truly is, and I refuse to let them find out by me ripping their mother to shreds in a fit of fury.

Once I step down, my secrets will be safe.

I'll make sure of it.

ONE

Ares

THE AIR IN TYNEWOOD IS ALIVE WITH ELECTRICITY and promise. A new school term is starting. Senior year at Tynewood University, and I can't wait to see what the next few months hold. This small town that sits a stone's throw away from the Olympic National Forest is picturesque, yet it's filled with secrets because of the Gilded Sovereign secret society, which has educated the most influential people in the country.

I'm not sure why the ancestors, my ancestors chose this town to start the Sovereign, but all the whispers I've heard about it have confirmed the founding families are born of

10

European royalty. Before I was born, even before my father or grandfather.

The university has given birth to presidents, statesmen, and the families who live in Tynewood all come from blue blood. Royalty. Which explains more or less how the Gilded Sovereign got its name.

My mind is on the upcoming initiation. I haven't been officially welcomed into the society yet, but in a week, on my twenty-first birthday, I'll be given the cloak, crown, and tattoo, along with access to contacts around the world. Each one is a connection to more money and power.

Inked on my flesh forever will be the royal symbol of the Gilded Sovereign. My ancestors created it and the legacy will soon be mine. My future is held in the hands of a secret society. And I have plans. The moment I'm sworn in, I'll seek my revenge.

With the power the Sovereign allows me, I'll be able to finally get vengeance on the asshole who's haunted my dreams since I was sixteen. I wanted to find him then, to make him pay, but my father assured me that nothing good would come of it.

I had to wait.

But patience is not my virtue.

I pull up to the university and take note of the new students all milling around the entrance. It's as if they're afraid to step inside and rightly so. This place is haunted with ghosts of the ancestors who built it. At least, that's what the residents of Tynewood tell anyone new who moves here.

Fear is one emotion that's been eradicated from me. Forced out of me since I was a child. At sixteen, I bore witness to my mother's murder, which has desensitized me from the violence of the world. Perhaps it's the blood that runs through my veins—blue blood.

As a Lancaster, our family has a history in this town, and it goes back all the way to the fucking eighteen hundreds. I can never escape who I am, or what I am, but that's where the beauty lies, I never want to. I've accepted the man I am.

When I turned eighteen, my father finally

explained it all, told me the truth about what will be expected of me. He knew I wouldn't refuse. The night my mother was murdered, I vowed I'd kill the man who did it, and Dad promised he'd help me. I want to make him proud.

The only way to get my revenge is to have the backing of the society. They can sweep anything under the rug, whether it's violence, bribery, or an illicit affair.

The Lancaster name will always be whispered throughout the town, throughout the hallways of Tynewood University. I'm proud of my heritage, no matter how bloody and violent it is, it's who I am. It's my birthright.

Shoving the door of my Maserati open, I exit the vehicle and glance around. It's fall, and the air is heavy with the promise of winter. I enjoy the cold, the rain… it calms me.

"There he is." My best friend and confidante, Etienne Durand, saunters up to me with his confident swagger. His ancestors, like mine, are one of the founding families in this town. And he'll soon be beside me as we're initiated into the Gilded Sovereign.

"I see the fresh meat has arrived," I remark, taking in the freshmen all huddled in the corner of the quad. Blondes, brunettes, redheads, even blue-haired beauties fill the space.

"Fuck yeah, man," Etienne chuckles, slapping me on the shoulder in camaraderie. "And this weekend we're going to party," he informs me, with a grin of mischievousness. Every year, we throw a welcome party for the new students. And every year, I make sure I have one pretty girl, in particular, I focus on.

They all fall into the trap I set—taunting and teasing them—and when I break their hearts, the pleasure is all mine. It's a sick game I play, but I can't bring myself to stop.

It's all part of being royalty.

I can do whatever I want.

"Who's that?" Tarian, the third in our trio, saunters up beside me, nudging his chin in the direction of a pretty dark-haired vixen. She's a head shorter than me, her hair hangs down to her tailbone, and she's dressed like a tomboy.

Chucks, a pair of skinny jeans, and a *too-big* tee.

But it's her full, pouty lips that grab my attention. She's smiling at her friend, a pretty blonde. Even though she looks like she's happy, her stance is rigid, as if she's tense about something. We could put it down to first day nerves, or could it be something else?

"I want to find out," I tell him, still eyeing up the beauty that's caught my attention. "Let's go, I have to get to class before that asshole, Harding loses his shit." My sneer is evident, and the frustration in my tone is clear. Professor Harding is one of the history professors who heads up the department. And he's also one of the Elder Crowns, one of the men I have to keep happy.

I'm spending the year as his Teaching Assistant when he needs me. Even though I have classes of my own to attend, I'll be offering my free time to Harding because Dad has made sure I behave this year.

Last year, I rebelled, I fought back at every turn, but when he told me I would step up as a

Crown of the Sovereign, I tampered down my rage and focused on revenge instead.

Etienne, Tarian, and I need to prove ourselves to the Elder Crowns who will initiate us and vote us in. We need to show them we're capable of running the society. The age to join used to be eighteen, but they changed it two years ago because of young, hotheaded assholes who caused some shit by spewing information about the society in a Vegas strip club breaking the society's most absolute law—never speak of the Sovereign to any outsiders.

Harding doesn't like me very much, and the feeling is mutual. I wasn't meant to be one of the Crowns, but as the rules stand, since he doesn't have a son, I'll take a seat at the table. The Sovereign is rigid in the *no women* rule.

"We'll do a walkthrough later, get some introductions done," I tell my best friends. Both understand why I want this so badly. They're both firstborn sons, which means they automatically get in, I have a bit of extra work to do to take my rightful place in the

Sovereign.

"I'll see you tonight," Etienne tells me as he heads off to his class, leaving me with Tar.

After offering Etienne a nod before he disappears, I turn to my left. "You coming tonight?"

Tarian glances at me with bright blue eyes that match the sky today. "What's happening tonight?" He questions as he pulls out a packet of smokes, tapping one out before placing it between his lips.

"We're meeting down at the lake house," I tell him, "I'm thinking of having a little get together. The calm before the storm."

Orientation week is one of the busiest at the school, especially for the freshmen. The seniors tend to hide out at the Lancaster lake house, which sits on the edge of town behind the forest. It's secluded and tranquil, something I think I'll be needing before my rigorous course load begins.

"Yeah." Tar grins. "Let's get a few girls out there. I need to get my dick wet." This time, he chuckles, and I just shake my head.

"You know it," I respond, fist-bumping him before making it up the stairs and toward my class. Even though I settle in my chair, attempting to focus, my mind is still on the fresh meat that's arrived. The one with hair the color of night. Something about her has me intrigued.

"Welcome back, minions," Professor Harding greets us. In his late fifties, he's one of the oldest staff members at the school. Also, one of the Crowns of the Sovereign.

His gaze lands on me within seconds of his greeting, his stare hardening into narrows slits before he turns his attention back to the rest of the students.

"This year, you'll be obeying my every command because I'm not going easy on you." His snark is clear. Asshole thinks he runs the world. "Since it's the first day of your final year at Tynewood, I was thinking about taking it easy on you, but... I'm not that nice. Remember, I'm the one who makes sure you pass your finals. Anything less than an A in my class is a fail."

A groan resounds in the room, and he smiles. The darkness this man exudes is worse than my father's domineering demeanor. Harding is the same age as Dad, but he looks ten times older. He acts it, too.

"Now, let's have a little fun and talk about what we remember from last year." He grins before lifting a stack of pages, which makes me think we have a goddamn pop quiz.

Muffled complaints echo around me, but that only makes him happier. Sitting back in my seat, I pull out my cell phone and tap out a message to Dad, who I know is at work down the hall. As a history professor, he takes pride in his class, in his students, and I know I'm stirring shit between him and Harding, but that's why I'm here—to shake up an age-old society that needs new blood.

TWO

Dahlia

My heart thuds against my chest as I meander through the throng of students. I'm out of my depth, but I can't deny that mingled with the anxiety is excitement.

Tynewood is a small town, with the university that my dad attended sitting in the center, taking up most of the town. Since his death a month ago, I moved here, hoping to find some semblance of family with my gran, my dad's mother.

My father's mother, Beatrice Milton, is a homebody, just like me. She's never left the small town she was born in, and she never once visited us in D.C. Her house is beautiful, with two bedrooms, one now mine, she's looked after the property since she and my late grandfather moved in when they were newlyweds.

Gran's still a stranger to me, but I hope living with her will bring us closer, and I'll get to know her better. Focusing on the looming buildings ahead of me, I can't help but feel nervous. Everything about this town is new to me, and even though I grew up in a bustling city, something about the size of Tynewood makes me anxious.

Thankfully, my best friend, Rukaiya, will be attending school with me. When she begged her dad to let her stay with me, he decided to move here with her. I'm still not sure why, it seemed strange at the time, but now that we're both here, I'm happy to have someone I know close by.

And I feel slightly less alone than I did in the big city.

As I head toward the grassy quad, I spin on my heel, trying to figure out where I'm supposed to go next. Each class I walk into is intimidating. There are so many students. Who would've thought a small town can house this many people? Fear trickles through me at the thought of doing all this without my father guiding me.

When I was growing up, he would be the one to offer advice, to tell me where to go, how to act. I suppose, since I'm nineteen, I should be used to being on my own, being independent, and I guess I am to a certain extent, but my stomach has been coiled tight since I woke up this morning.

Glancing at my schedule, I take note of my next class and turn in a circle in an attempt to find the building I'm meant to be heading toward, but confusion settles like a lead weight in my gut.

"Lost, pretty girl?" The question comes from behind me, causing me to pivot into the hard body of a boy... no, a man. Definitely not a freshman. Broad shoulders encased in a black shirt that looks a little too tight around the biceps. His torso tapers toward hips and thighs in torn dark jeans.

"I... Uhm..." My words are stuck in my throat when I trail my stare back up into eyes the color of a cloudless day—bright and luminous, shimmering with mischief.

"Don't be scared," he quips. "I won't bite, well… not unless you ask me to, then I'll gladly oblige." His baby blue eyes sparkle and I find myself relaxing somewhat.

"This place is a maze to me."

"Let's see," he says, tugging the page from my trembling fingers and scanning the information. "Ah, you have good old Harding today." Something about the way he says this doesn't give me confidence in my next class.

"Is that a good or a bad thing?" I quip, trying to calm my erratic heartbeat. The guy is gorgeous. His eyebrows are black, along with his cropped hair, a stark contrast to the smooth pale skin that makes the tips of my fingers tingle to feel him—to feel if he's sculpted from porcelain with his sharp features and chiseled jaw. When he tips his head to the side, an unruly strand of onyx hair falls across his left eye, teasing the piercing that twinkles in the sunlight.

His full lips quirk into a grin, making the

ring through his lower lip glint at me. "Mmm.
. . Depends," he chuckles, gripping my
shoulder and turning me toward the left-wing
of the looming building. He starts walking,
leading me closer to the wooden door that's
sitting wide open at the moment.

"Depends on?" My question comes out
croaky, my nerves twisting as the heat of his
fingertips burn into me.

He doesn't respond, merely makes his
way toward the opening to my history class.
Students file into the classroom. The stranger,
holding onto my arm, stops, holds out his
hand, and I take my schedule from his strong
fingers.

"If you like an asshole who thinks he's
god's gift to this earth." This time, the smile
I'm met with makes my stomach somersault
wildly. Dimples peek out from both cheeks as
he regards me.

"I don't actually," I retort, causing him to
chuckle.

"Then you'll enjoy the rest of your year."
He doesn't wait for me to respond before he

24

starts walking away. I watch his retreating back, and I'm about to turn away when he stops. "Be careful of who you trust here," the alluring stranger tells me before he's swallowed by the crowd of students who make their way toward the door where I'm standing.

I didn't catch his name.

But I have a feeling I'll be seeing him again.

The moment I walk into the house, I find it empty. I wonder if Gran is at the library down the road. She mentioned it's one of her favorite places, and I forgot to tell her I'd like to visit it as well.

But, first things first, I need to get my textbooks ready for tomorrow's classes. Today was uneventful, except for the handsome guy who walked me to History class. I didn't see him again, and I have to admit, I was disappointed.

In the kitchen, I set a mug under the Keurig and press the button for a strong black coffee. The inky liquid trickles into the porcelain mug as I replay the events of the day in my mind. Five classes and all of them felt overwhelming. Doubt settles deep in my gut; I don't know if I can actually do this.

I'm so different from most of the kids at school, mainly because they've spent their entire lives in this town, and because I just moved here, I feel like the outsider looking into their perfect world and not knowing where I fit.

Picking up the mug, I inhale the mocha scent and will myself to focus on what I have to do this year—get through the next twelve months. It's not going to be easy, I can see that now. I'm used to living in a city where nobody knows me, but I can tell, just being here for a few days, that this town sticks together.

I close my eyes and recall the incident at lunch.

"She's new." The dark-haired girl glares at

me, making it known that she doesn't like me. Her hair is the color of raven's wings. Her big blue eyes shimmer with confidence as she looks me over.

I'm not one of the rich kids from Tynewood.

I grew up in the city, and even though my father wasn't struggling, and I had everything my heart desired. I'm no longer that girl, which frustrates me because I prefer being in a city where I'm one in a few million, not someone that sticks out like a sore thumb.

"She is indeed," her friend sneers, but I focus on my lunch and not the leering gazes that attempt to burn through me.

"Hey," Rukaiya's voice sounds happy, excited even. "I got this." She shoves a flyer over the table. The black, gold and red colors of the designs pop from the page.

"A party?"

"Yeah," Rukaiya shrugs. "You said you wanted to be more outgoing. This is the perfect opportunity." My best friend winks before pulling out a can of some new energy drink.

"Were you invited? Or did you find this lying around on a desk?" I ask with a smile. Something tells me my best friend would do anything to get me out of my bedroom.

"Stop being a party pooper, I was actually given this by a cute boy," she whispers as she leans in. Her gaze darting around, and I wonder if she's looking for said 'cute boy.'

"And he has nothing to do with you dragging me out?"

Rukaiya grins slyly, but she doesn't respond. She's tried to set me up with guys when we were in high school all the time, and the last time was the worst. I fell for Joshua and lost my virginity to him, then found out he was hitting on the captain of the cheerleading team only a day later.

"I just don't want you to become an old maid." Rukaiya laughs. "I mean, you're going to turn into that old lady with fifteen cats."

"I will not," I pout, crossing my arms in front of my chest. "I go out." My indignation earns me an eye roll from my best friend. "Okay, well, I mean sometimes."

"Come on, sugar cube," Rukaiya pleads, using the nickname she gave me when we first met. "You gotta have some fun."

"It's difficult when I can't stop thinking that my dad would want me to focus on school. I want to make him proud, Rukaiya."

Her smile falls, and the guilt creases her pretty face. "I'm sorry, Dahl," she says. "These are your college years. I just don't want you to be stuck indoors for the next four years."

Sighing, I nod. She's right. I would hide out in my bedroom if I could. "I know."

The two snobs, who were glaring at me earlier, notice the flyer. "The party is for elite only, outsiders aren't welcome."

Rukaiya's gaze locks on the dark-haired bitch. "I didn't realize elite meant whores who can't do their makeup," my best friend retorts angrily as she pushes up to stand.

The dark-haired girl sneers, before turning away from us. She strolls up to the football team, curling herself around one of the guys. I thought we left this mean girl syndrome back in high school, I guess I was wrong.

"Bitch."

"You could've just ignored her."

Rukaiya pins her glare on me. "No, I couldn't

have because I don't deal well with rude bitches."

"I don't know if this party is such a good idea." I meet Rukaiya's intense gaze. She's not letting this go, the conviction in her stare is enough to have me buckling.

"You're going. We're going. I'm not going to let idiots spoil our time in Tynewood. I came all this way for you," Rukaiya reminds me.

When I told her I'd be living with my gran in Tynewood and attending the university here, she begged her dad to send her here as well. What we didn't expect was her father to move them both here.

"Fine," I sigh in resignation. "One party. That's it."

"Of course." She giggles with a wink before grabbing her backpack. "I gotta get to the restroom before class. See ya." And I'm alone with my thoughts once more.

Which, at times, isn't always a good thing.

THREE

Ares

As soon as the sky darkens from a deep, fiery orange to a haunting, sinful black, I step out of the house and into the courtyard in front of our home. The Lancaster mansion sits on a hill that overlooks the town of Tynewood as if we're royalty watching over our subjects.

Slipping into the driver's seat of my Maserati, I turn the engine, and soon, I'm flying down the drive toward the gates of our estate. The night time has always been calming for me, but there are times when memories take over, and I would rather be basking in the sunshine.

Turning on the stereo, I turn up the volume, hoping to get lost in the music. A deep, heavy bass vibrates around me, reminding me that I have places to be and people to see. My phone rings in a shrill tone over the music, and I have to cut it before tapping the green button.

"Dad," I answer, wondering when he'll be leaving again. I prefer it when he's not in town. His job has him traveling to various cities and countries, and I wonder if it keeps his mind off mom's death.

"Ares, I have a job for you. Complete it, and I'll gift you something you've wanted for a very long time. But I need you to do this without starting a fucking war," he grits out. "Am I understood?"

"Yes, father."

"I need you to look into him. My office is open to you if you need it. If you can get all the information with a background check, perhaps I'll start giving you more responsibility. This is a time-sensitive task."

For my father to ask this of me means that he trusts me. I spent my teenage years trying to prove myself to the man. Since I was sixteen, I wanted him to trust me, to see me as a man, not a child. I always wished one day, I could be just like him—powerful and respected. And now that he's given me the go-ahead to walk into the office he deems as sacred, I can't help but smile.

"Who is he?" I ask as I turn toward the forest and step on the gas.

"Milton's partner, there's been news from D.C." My father's tone sounds wary as if he's hiding something. The name Milton makes me want to kill. The asshole murdered my mother, and he needs to pay. Rage fuels me as I spin into the parking lot and hit the brakes.

"What news?"

"I'm waiting on confirmation, but Milton is presumed dead." There's a hint of something in that same concealing tone, and I wonder if my father decided to take away the one thing, he promised me. Ice fills my veins at my father's revelation. My white-knuckle grip on the steering wheel tightens. He was meant to be mine. I wanted to take his life, slowly and painfully. I wanted to watch the asshole beg for mercy, and when he did, I would've sliced him limb from limb.

"What do you mean presumed dead? He was mine to finish."

"I'll be back home in the morning, we'll talk then," my father's hasty response makes me even more wary as to what he's hiding. If there's one thing I've learned about Abner Lancaster, it's that he's a master of hiding shit from his family.

"I'm at the lake house," I tell him. "I'll be home before you are, but I'll do a remote login from here."

"Thank you, son. And remember, whatever happens, you'll get your vengeance." He hangs up before I can respond. It's been far too long, and I've been patient. Only because he told me I had to wait. Generally, I don't obey the old man, but this time, I knew I had to. It's my ticket into the Sovereign. My 'in' to get that crown.

Shoving open my car door, I step out of the vehicle, before pulling in a lung full of the clean air. And even though it's beautiful, with the thick forest and silver lake, there's a dark history that's hidden within the walls of the university, and the town itself.

A rumbling engine alerts me that either Etienne or Tarian has arrived. Seconds later, a silver BMW SUV pulls up beside me. In the passenger seat is my biggest mistake and the driver is the asshole I call *brother*.

Don't get me wrong, I love Philipe, but, at times, his choices can be questionable, case in point, the fact that he has Kelli in his car. She offers me a finger wiggling wave before my brother opens her door. Used to being treated like a princess, she's been a pain in my ass since I threw her out after a few nights of debauchery.

"Hey, Ares," she grins as if it's going to get her on my dick again. Not a chance in hell.

Folding my arms in front of my chest, I pin her with a glare. "What are you doing here?" Philipe takes a step toward me, giving me a look that says not to ask. But I don't obey my fucking brother. "I didn't think you were that desperate to have another Lancaster inside you," I taunt, knowing she's going to go running to Philipe.

"Cut it out," he grits as he tugs the cooler from the trunk of his car.

I don't need this shit. Spinning on my heel, I make for the house and unlock it before stepping inside. The musty air is the only evidence that we haven't been here in months. Each summer we would come out here and spend our vacation at the lake. But over time, the tradition died off, and when Philipe moved to New York and my father was away, I started my own tradition of sorts.

Party at the lake.

I make my way directly to the floor to ceiling windows and push open the sliding doors, which lead out onto the patio. The sky is ink with pinpricks of white. The moon is high, a sliver of silver against a backdrop of darkness.

My favorite time of the day, when the sun hides and the shadows come to play. More cars arrive, but I don't go inside, I don't acknowledge that my brother brought my ex. Voices filter through the house, and glasses clink in the kitchen.

"You hiding out," Etienne greets when he joins me. Dressed in a pair of blue jeans and a black Guns N' Roses' tee, he looks relaxed.

"I am, Philipe decided having Kelli here would be a good idea. Asshole." My best friend chuckles at me. It's been a long while since I ran from a woman, but Kelli is a viper, and I don't know what my brother is doing with her, but if he's into sloppy seconds, he can have at it.

"I wonder if the new girls will be here," Etienne says before he sips the beer he's holding. He watches me with the dark glass bottle pressed against his lips.

"No newbies. I didn't tell anyone unless Tarian's decided he wants to get his dick wet." I grin. Even though Etienne is our equivalent of Casanova, it's Tarian who brings all the beauties along with him whenever there's a party. He lives his life as if it's his last day on earth.

Perhaps it's time we all took a page from his book. The music blares to life as the girls squeal in the house. I can't stop rolling my eyes when Kelli comes outside to drape herself over Etienne.

"Hey, E." She smiles up at him. He's probably two heads taller than her. She's a tiny little black-haired minx who would jump on any dick if it meant she'd be a part of the in-crowd. And that's why I said she's my biggest mistake and my last regret.

"Didn't know you'd be here," he tells her, shrugging her off his arm, which causes her to scowl. Her fat, pouty lips purse in frustration when she steps back.

"Guess Philipe is the only one with some taste here," she scoffs, glancing over at me.

I lift my drink, tipping it toward her, before responding. "Guess so. My brother is well known for taking sloppy seconds," I bite out just to annoy the fuck out of her.

"Fuck you, Ares. When you wanted me, I was always there for you."

"Yeah, to spread your legs," I retort back with a chuckle.

She bristles at my words, and I know she's pissed off. She'll probably run to her daddy to complain about me, and if it gets back to Harding, it will definitely get back to my father. But right now, I'm not in the fucking mood for her bullshit.

Kelli spins on her heel and makes her way inside, leaving Etienne and me to stare at the tiny shorts that hug her bubble butt.

"She does look good in those," my best friend grumbles, and I can't deny he's right. The shoes she's wearing accentuate every part of her muscled calves and thighs.

"Yeah, but she ain't worth the headache."

"*She* might be," Etienne's gaze is captured by someone inside the house, and I turn to find a blonde who's dressed in denim cut-offs, black fishnets, and a torn tank top that reads, *Bitch*, on the front across her tits.

"Go for it," I slap him on the back, giving his shoulder a squeeze before I head up the side of the house to the private second floor. It's my getaway when shit gets too much downstairs, and I've always enjoyed the peace and quiet that it offers.

The vibration from downstairs still thuds

through the floor, but the giggles and squeals are dimmed somewhat as I push through the glass door and flop on the sofa. The bottle of bourbon I left here a couple of months ago still sits on the coffee table.

I twist it open and pour a double shot into one of the tumblers and gulp down the fiery liquid. When I get a refill, I hear a harsh screech and the splash of water that follows tells me people are already in the lake.

Pushing off the sofa, I head to the window to see who's down there. Tarian's arrived, and he's standing with the blonde who Etienne was staring at, and beside her is the raven-haired beauty who caught my attention at school earlier.

"Well, hello, flower," I smile, sipping my drink. As if she can feel my eyes on her, she spins around, her gaze trailing all over the house until they reach the window where I'm standing, but she can't see me through the one-sided window.

Her friend captures her attention, and she smiles, the movement tilting her full lips, crinkling her nose, and making her eyes sparkle like dark gemstones under the lamp that they're standing in front of.

Even in the dark, I can tell there's something about this girl. Something dangerous. And I can't help but swallow my drink and smile. Turning to the room, I head to the desk and open the laptop I keep here for when I need to study.

Once I'm logged in, I open the software Tarian built for my dad and tap in the name he sent in the email.

Fergus Harrison.

Why the fuck would he come all the way to Tynewood?

Hitting enter, I wait for the program to run with information. The screen fills with names, addresses, and connections to the name. Nothing particularly interesting pops up, and I wonder briefly if Dad is sending me off on a wild goose chase. I'm not sure why he would, but something isn't sitting right with me.

Once the pages are printed out, I shove them into a folder and clip it closed. Shutting down the laptop, I ensure everything is as it was before I walked in. I rise, glancing around me once more before I head down to my car to hide the documents.

As soon as I know they're safe, I'll head to the party.

Time to get fucked up.

FOUR

Dahlia

We've just come inside after my best friend decided that gulping down shots as if it were her last day on earth was a good idea. "I'm not feeling so good," Rukaiya mutters in my ear.

I hold onto her arm, trying to get her attention as she curls over and coughs. "Do you want to leave?" I ask her, worried she may have alcohol poisoning. Surely, she would've had to drink a lot more than she did. But I have no idea. I've only ever had a few sips of wine with dinner when Dad deemed it acceptable.

Rukaiya nods, looking up at me, and I shake my head. I knew we should've stayed home. This is the reason I'm not a fan of parties.

Leading her from the house, I make my way to the car and open the passenger seat, allowing her to slip inside. I'm rounding the front when the dark-haired guy comes running up to us.

"Hey," he smiles at me, "leaving so soon?"

"She's not feeling too good," I tell him, pointing at Rukaiya in the car before turning toward him again.

"I'm sorry," he says, and it seems as if he's genuinely sorry. "Is there anything I can do? I can drive you?" In the barely-there light, the piercing in the center of his full bottom lip blinks, catching my attention.

"No, it's okay. I have my car, and I haven't had anything to drink," I tell him with a smile.

"Before you go, I wanted to introduce myself properly. I'm Tarian," he holds out his hand, and I can't help slipping mine in his and shaking.

"I'm Dahlia," I tell him with a grin. "I'm sorry we're such lightweights."

"Oh, that's no problem. Just promise me you'll be at the party on Saturday," He hands me a flyer, which is the same as the one that Rukaiya had earlier at lunch.

"Uhm... I don't know—"

Tarian leans in closer, his gaze holding mine hostage and I can't look away. He smells of mint and cinnamon. And a hint of whiskey. "Come on, you'd make me a very happy guy if you would come," he winks playfully, and I can't stop the blush I know is forming on my cheeks.

"Ha, nice line. Does that work on all the girls?"

"All the time." His overconfidence makes me laugh out loud as my gaze drifts from him for a second, landing on the doorway where a guy is staring out at us. His gaze locks on me.

Tarian notices my distraction and turns toward the house. "Oh, don't worry about him. Just ignore my friend, he's a little intense sometimes."

"Looks it."

"So, you'll come on Saturday?" He asks again. He's definitely a charmer. There's something sweet about him, and he's not rude at all, not like that asshole in the doorway glaring at me.

"Sure, yeah." I finally nod.

"Awesome," he says with a grin, which accentuates his dimples. "See you then, pretty girl." He turns and leaves me at the car, and my attention is once more caught on the man in the doorway. His hands stuck in his jean pockets, his dark hair and face shadowed. When he moves, I get a glimpse of his face, which is almost sculpture perfect.

He turns and shuts the door behind him after Tarian disappears inside, and I'm shaken. I'm not sure what it is about him, but I don't like the way he was looking at me. Perhaps it's my imagination playing tricks on me. Or maybe there's more to the stranger in the darkness than meets the eye.

Slipping into the driver's seat, I start the car and pull out of the parking spot, which really is just a large open area in front of the lake house. The high trees swallow us up as I pull onto the road and away from the mansion that overlooks silver water. Even though it's not far from town, it seems like it's nestled in the middle of nowhere.

With a quick glance to my left, I find my best friend passed out in the seat beside me, so I don't turn on the music.

Instead, my mind replays the strange interaction with Tarian and the stranger from the doorway. I should've asked what his name is, but I was far too shaken to think about it. His glare heated every inch of me in ways I don't think I want to explore right now.

In the silence, I wonder if I'll see him tomorrow.

Would he be as threatening in the light?

It only takes us fifteen minutes to reach Rukaiya's house. I kill the engine and exit the car. Once I've opened her door, I shake her awake, startling her for a second. When my best friend realizes where she is, she smiles sheepishly.

"I'm sorry for ruining your party," she tells me.

"Trust me, it wasn't my party." Shaking my head, I help her to stand, before shutting the door. "I'm happy to go home and get lost in a new book."

Rukaiya rolls her eyes, and I know she's about to make fun of me for my love of books. "You know, book boyfriends aren't going to keep you warm at night," she tells me with a wink.

"Yeah, they can, I have an overactive imagination," I retort. "And I have many book boyfriends who will keep me all cuddly and warm." This time, we both fall into a fit of giggles.

"Yeah, yeah," my best friend says. "Next party is on Saturday, and I'll be ready. You're going to meet some hottie, and you'll forget all about those boys in your books." She presses a kiss to my cheek before heading inside her house.

I watch for a moment before I slip back into my car and turn the engine. It's only a few minutes before I'm home and pulling into the driveway behind Gran's old Toyota. When I step into the house, the smell of freshly baked bread and soup assaults my senses, and my stomach growls.

"I guess my girl is hungry?" Gran smiles

from the doorway that leads into the kitchen. Even though it's late, she's been cooking for me.

"I am. Thanks, Gran," I tell her, leaving my phone and keys on the dining room table before following her into the kitchen where there are two large bowls she's filling with soup and a loaf of bread waiting to be devoured.

I sit on one of the chairs, grabbing a spoon, and scoop soup into the metal utensil. The scent of vegetables is overwhelming, and I take my first sip, savoring the peppery flavor.

"I've added quite a bit of black pepper, it's good for this cold weather," Gran tells me. Winter is on its way, and I'm not looking forward to it. My dad told me about how snowy, and cold Tynewood gets.

"Thanks for this."

"You're home early," Gran remarks, glancing at the large wooden clock that hangs above the doorway to the hall.

Nodding, I cut a slice of bread before answering, "Rukaiya wasn't feeling well."

"How much did she have to drink?" My grandmother doesn't miss a thing, and I can't help but smile. Even though we're considered adults, she still worries about us.

"A few shots of something or the other. I was driving so I didn't have any."

Gran shakes her head as she joins me at the table. We eat in silence, which only has my mind reeling back to the moment with the guy in the doorway at the Lakehouse. Tarian is sweet and friendly, but there was something about the stranger who stood in the shadows. A magnetism that attempted to pull me in closer. And I wanted to go to him, to see him up close, but I have a feeling I'll be seeing him soon enough if he's attending university with Tarian.

"Your mind ain't here tonight, young lady," Gran remarks when she finishes her soup and sits back to regard me with those silver-blue eyes. My dad had the same eyes, but I look more like my mother. Everyone used to tell me I was the spitting image of her.

"I'm just tired. I think," I tell her.

"No cute boys at the party?" She grins, waggling her eyebrows.

Shaking my head, I laugh at her attempt to interrogate me. "Gran, I'm not having boy talk with you."

"Why not? I was young once." She chuckles, holding her glass of wine and tipping it toward me before taking a mouthful.

"Well... I mean there was Tarian, but I don't know his last name."

"Calvert," she responds.

"You know him?" This has my attention, and she smiles fondly as if she knows him well.

Gran nods. "I do. Known that boy since before he could walk. The Calvert's are one of the original families in Tynewood. If he was there, then you'd have met Ares and Etienne as well."

"Mmm." I furrow my brows, thinking about the name of the guy who was all over Rukaiya. "Yes, Etienne was trying to get Rukaiya to go out with him. But I don't recall an Ares."

She considers my answer then shakes her head once more. "Ares is difficult. He's been in trouble more times than I can count."

"Why?" Something tells me this is the stranger in the doorway, and now more than ever, I want to meet this troublemaker.

"He's a bad boy, and you steer clear of him." She waggles her finger at me as if I were a child getting into trouble. "Our families don't get along well," Gran tells me, with a hint of sadness in her tone. "There's an old family war, which hasn't been settled."

My ears perk up at this information, and I'm on the edge of my seat, wanting to know more. "What kind of war?"

Gran shakes her head. "A cruel one. That's all you need to know. Stay away from him." She rises, grabbing both bowls to place in the dishwasher, and with her back turned, I figure that this is the last I'll hear of it from her.

Perhaps I should get the story from the source.

From Ares himself.

Now I just need to find him.

FIVE

Ares

A FIST SLAMS INTO MY MIDSECTION, CAUSING A groan to fall from my lips. The asshole in front of me thinks he's got me beat, but this time, it's me who's about to pummel him. Tarian and Etienne are shouting my name as the rest of the crowd screams for the man I'm fighting.

Blood drips onto my tongue, and I turn rabid. My fists make contact with his face, his jaw, and then his forehead, taking the fucker down in five easy punches. The metallic stench hangs heavily in my nostrils when I inhale deeply. It's the fragrance of winning. It's what I do, and I revel in it.

I'm pushed and pulled, being gripped and hugged, but when I meet Billy's stare, he offers a nod. I've just won him a lot of money.

Not that he needs it. He takes the money from the rich, drunk motherfuckers who bet on two men beating each other to a pulp on a worn-out floor mat and donates it all to charities across the country.

When the crowd thins, I head to Billy, who's leaning against the makeshift bar, and grab the beer he's offering. Tarian and Etienne join us, settling on the stools along the counter.

"Good fight," B grins, waving a wad of cash in his face. He plays the role of a struggling gym owner well. Most of the men here don't really know he lives on the outskirts of town in a mansion, a few hectares of land, and owns at least five sports cars and three SUVs.

"Yeah, he wasn't too much hassle." Swiping the sweat from my brow with the towel, I glance at my best friends. "Ready for tomorrow?"

They know what I mean, the party that's being hosted at my house needs to be planned in fine detail. Mainly because every time I have a party, my father returns and finds the place in disarray.

This time, however, I know he'll be away until Monday, which gives us until Sunday night to perfectly polish the mansion from top to bottom.

"All good. No changes in our party schedule." Etienne's grin is contagious, and my mouth tilts into a smile as well.

"You gotta be careful. You father isn't a man to mess with," Billy warns me again. He's always been there for me. Each time I walk into his gym and the back room where we're now standing, it's given me the confidence that I lacked due to a father who only doted on his eldest son.

But now that I'll be named as one of the Crowns, soon, I'll be at the table alongside Philipe, and there's nothing my father can do to stop it. The Sovereign is in my blood, in my very DNA. I was born a Lancaster -- the founding family of the town and of the society.

"I'm a big boy now, B-man," I tell him. "I'm a Crown, I'm also a Lancaster, and nobody fucks with me."

"Even your father?" His challenge makes

my teeth clench. Frustration ebbs and flows, but I can't get angry because it's true. Abner is the only man who's ever had me scared. But not anymore.

"I'll be all cleaned up by the time Dad sees me again," I tell him, swiping the crimson from my lip. The harsh flavor fills my mouth, and I swallow it back. I'm not afraid of a little blood.

How can a warrior of war cower when he sees the crimson of battle?

He can't, and I'm ready to walk on the front line.

"He won't give in easily." I know Billy is right, but then again, he hasn't seen me in action.

"See ya around, B-man."

When we exit the gym, I slip into the driver's seat of my SUV and turn the engine. Tarian follows behind while Etienne leads from the front. I'm in the center, so if one of my father's minions were following me, we'd scope him out.

An email comes through, lighting the

screen of my phone. It catches my attention. News about Dahlia, which only makes me think of the perfect, pristine flower again. Perhaps I should take the time to visit her tonight.

Pulling into the driveway of the Lancaster estate, I kill the engine and get out, meeting Tarian and Etienne on the cobblestones, which lead up to the front door.

"I'm thinking about paying Dahlia a visit later," I inform them as we make our way up the steps. I can feel both of them staring at me, but I can't face them. I don't want to admit that I find her hot as fuck, that I want to learn more about her.

It frustrates me that she's so beautiful. That she's so alluring. She's on my mind all day, every day, and most nights, too. Even after the fight, I'm still tense. My muscles ache from the exertion, but it feels good.

"Are you sure that's a good idea?" Etienne

questions from my left. When I met him in middle school, he told me I was an asshole after we had an argument about who had the best-packed lunch. He'd only said the curse word because he heard his mom call his dad that and thought it was cool.

We got into trouble that day because the teacher heard him, and we both got pulled into detention. We made a pact that if one of us goes down, the other does, too.

In high school, Etienne was like a goddamned manwhore. He lost his virginity to an older woman, but he's never told us her name. All we know about her is that she's a cougar who loves her boy toys. After that, his confidence grew, and the cheerleaders, emo chicks, and even the debate, society fell over their heels for him.

He knows what women want to hear. It's as if he was born with a silver tongue and a golden dick. That's Etienne.

Not long after meeting Etienne, Tarian joined the school after his folks moved back to Tynewood, and the three of us became inseparable. Tarian's parents died in a tragic accident two years after moving to Tynewood, which left Tarian under the guardianship of his uncle. The uncle who ran off to England and doesn't care if his nephew is dead or alive.

I glance at Etienne and finally offer him an answer, "No. Probably not, but, then again, you know me. When am I ever one to do something because it's good?"

"That's true."

"She's pretty and innocent. You won't have a problem with her at all," Tarian tells me. We always work together. When one of us needs something done, we all help out. Tarian offered to be the one to make contact with Dahlia, and I agreed.

He may not have the outright charm that Etienne has, but something about Tarian always sets girls at ease. I saw him last night when she left the party with her friend. And our plan worked because he invited her to the party on Saturday, and I know she accepted.

I can't wait for her to step foot into my home. I just wish I could lock her up and keep her here.

"I don't give a shit how innocent she is. I want to dirty up her pristine appearance." I chuckle, thinking about bending her over every surface in my house until she can't think about anything other than me. And once she falls for me, I'll rip her heart from her chest in front of the whole fucking town.

"You know, they say that the more sex you have, the better chance you have of retaining your memory when you're older," Etienne tells me as if he's reading my thoughts. His smirk is in place, and I know the moment I respond, he'll have some bullshit facts, which I don't want to know about right now.

"Isn't it past your curfew?" I bite out my response, frustration evident in my voice, which causes him to chuckle.

"Okay, kids, can we play nicely?" Tarian offers as he kicks my bedroom door shut. He pulls out a joint, which he rolled earlier, and flicks the lighter. The flame dances along the end of the smoke and the red cherry comes to life.

"He was being an asshole," I grin, flopping on the bed. I watch them take their respective seats: Tarian always in my desk chair, and Etienne in the bean bag he's always loved that's facing the balcony.

"I think we should bring her in. Tell her everything. She needs to know the truth," Tarian says before pulling in a lungful of smoke, coming toward me, he hands me the joint. I watch him blow smoke rings from his mouth before he continues, "She's a Crown."

"There's no place for women in the Sovereign."

"What if there was?" He challenges. What he's saying goes against everything I've been brought up to believe. My father would never allow us to Crown, a female. Not even Kelli is allowed to sit at the table.

"This is ridiculous. You know it will never happen." I inhale a deep lungful of smoke, my eyes closing as the hit takes hold of me for a moment longer. "And besides," I look at Etienne, "she'll never submit to me being in charge of her."

My best friends grin at me stupidly when I utter those words. I know they're thinking about it, taking the little flower and making her fall to her knees for our pleasure. What they don't know is, I will never share her. She's mine to toy with, her body will bend to *my* will only. I want her heart to shatter, and I want to be the one to break her.

"I gotta jet," Etienne says, rising from the bean bag and grabbing the last of the joint. Planting it between his lips, he offers us both a salute before he heads out the door. I know he'll be back in a few hours. Sleep doesn't come easy when you're about to give yourself over to a secret society.

"You want to come to the church with me?" I ask Tarian.

"I'm working on something for your dad," he tells me. "I have a feeling he's hiding something." His words shock me silent. "I'll tell you when I find out anything." He rises, making his way to the door. But he stops before he walks out. "Listen to me, Ares," he looks over his shoulder at me. "Be careful.

Your dad may be blood, but there's something not quite right with this situation."

Once I'm alone, Tarian's words tumble over in my head on replay, and I push off the bed as the buzz hits me. I shouldn't go there now, but even as I make my way down to my car, I smile when I think about seeing her.

Perhaps I should leave her alone for now. Until Saturday when she's in my house, within the walls of the Lancaster mansion. But I've never been one to think logically when it comes to revenge.

Slipping into the driver's seat, I press Start, causing the engine to purr to life. And as much as I want to turn down the road to her house, I don't. I make my way up the hill toward the church. When I pull onto the dirt road, it doesn't take long till I'm parking round the back and exiting the vehicle.

The moment I step foot into the abandoned building, I find the one pew that's still standing and settle on it. Leaning back, I allow the high from the joint to seep through my veins.

Dahlia's pretty face appears in my mind's

eye, and I focus on those wide blue eyes, plump pink lips, and her long dark hair. She's bad for me. I'm attracted to her, but she's not someone I can keep. Dahlia is here for me to finally seek the revenge I need.

That's all.

I don't know why, but there's a tether between us, and I'm about to tie it even tighter. I can't tell the guys about this because they won't understand. I've spent my life needing to hurt someone for my mother's death, and now that the chance has landed in my lap, I keep second guessing myself.

The memory of watching her father pull the trigger flits into my mind, and I'm on my feet, pacing back and forth. The silver light of the full moon shines through the broken window, and I stop to stare up at it.

"She will fucking pay."

It's a vow. One I intend to keep.

SIX

Dahlia

STARING AT MY REFLECTION, I TAKE IN MY LONG black hair that hangs in glossy waves down to the middle of my back. The color shimmers with gold highlights, reminding me of my mother when she would take me to the salon with her.

I haven't seen her in years.

I was eleven when she walked out and never looked back. At the time, I didn't understand why, but growing up with my father, I realized she wasn't leaving me as much as she was leaving him. My father was a difficult man to get along with mainly because of his job. And now that he's no longer here, now that I'm alone in the world, I wish she would come to find me.

I blink once, twice, and lean closer to the mirror to focus on the black liner that I swipe along the lid of my left eye. Once I get the swish, I continue with the right one. Even though my mother wasn't present when I wanted to learn about makeup, boys, and anything else I should've been able to ask her about, I had Rukaiya who guided me along the way.

My eyes are wide, the contacts making the ordinarily deep blue pop as if there is a flame dancing behind the irises. I'm all grown up now, and it's time I acted like it.

I'm excited about the party tonight, perhaps I'll see Tarian again; he was friendly. But even as I think this, my mind flits back to the guy in shadows who reminded me of a predator. As if he was about to attack me, stealing me in the dark and making me his.

A cold shiver trickles its way down my spine at the thought, and I try to push it away. Focusing on the mirror, I pull my hair into a hair tie.

Even though going tonight is not my idea of fun, I promised Rukaiya I'd be more outgoing. So, I'm going to have fun tonight and stop hiding my nose in my books.

"Dahlia, your friend is here," Gran calls from the hallway.

"Thanks, Gran." I smile, just as the door swings open, and I'm met with my best friend. She's all dolled up, and I wonder if I'm underdressed, even though I'm wearing a lot less than I usually would. I'm more at home in sweatpants and a tee. Dresses are the last thing on my list to wear.

"Are you ready?" Rukaiya's voice comes from the doorway, making me smile. Her blonde dreadlocks are shimmering with glitter, and I can't help laughing. "What?" she asks, scrunching her nose.

"You glitter bombed your hair?" I question, taking in the small glints each time she swishes her long hair left and right. She's one of the most beautiful girls I know. Her European heritage gives her a smooth alabaster skin tone, and her wide eyes are lighter than mine, almost silver.

"I figured I needed to look good. This

is our first *college* party," she tells me while arching her perfectly curved brow. Her dress hugs her hourglass figure in a dark charcoal material, which reminds me of silky spandex. *Is there such a thing?*

"I know, but you know what I'm like," I tell her on a sigh. We went to school together in Washington, and she was the only friend I had at school that my father actually liked. He approved of her because her father was his partner. Together, they caught bad guys; it was the connection between them that afforded me a connection with Rukaiya.

My father's job as an undercover cop was always something I feared. Deep down, I always wondered when he wouldn't come home from a job. He never got to spend much time with me, and his fear was always that I would end up hurt because people would find out his identity and mine.

My father had always kept me locked up. I was a bookworm by nature, so I didn't mind it. I got used to my own company. It's my norm, and even now, I can't understand why clubbing and partying is so popular. But then again, I live inside my own mind where fairytales and handsome boys *are* my *real life*.

If it weren't for me being a book worm, more interested in the boys between the pages than those at school, Dad would've locked me in a tower until I was an old maid, graying with one foot in the grave. The two men ruled our homes with an iron fist, not allowing us to go out unless we had our phone apps locked-on tracking, so they could find us if need be.

"You need to stop being a homebody, sugar," she coos. "Remember, you promised to let your hair down when we got here. It's time to live. Your dad..." her words taper off into nothing, and the pain that pangs against my chest steal my breath.

Shaking it off, I nod. She's right. I did say I would finally let myself enjoy the time I have here. I offer my best friend a smile and pull her in for a hug.

"Let's just go and have fun," I tell her. I'm thankful I have someone in my life to push me outside my comfort zone. "It's time for me to stop living in the fairytales I have been," I tell her, whispering, "And maybe, just maybe, I'll meet someone who can show me that life is worth living."

"That's what I like to hear." She winks playfully. "And hey," Rukaiya says, capturing my attention, as I move to the closet and pull it open. "Listen to me because I'm always right. You are going to meet some hot boy who's going to sweep you off your feet."

Her words have me laughing out loud. She knows how much I love my romance novels. I certainly talk about them often enough to have her wanting to know about the latest book, boyfriend.

"And, if I meet some weirdo, you're meant to save me. Best friend pact, right?" I question, my eyebrows raised as I regard her.

"Of course, I'll swoop in as any best friend should, and I'll knee him in the junk." We both fall into a fit of giggles. I've always had fun with her. Since the moment we met at school to the second she told me she wanted to attend Tynewood, I knew I'd have a friend forever.

She's been there for me through my worst and my best. Even when I had a crush on the football captain in high school, and he bullied me, I could always count on Rukaiya.

"And if you do meet some hottie," she informs me. "Make sure he has a best friend for me." It was our pact to always be there for each other, not only on the subject of boys but also when we were both at our lowest.

My eyes prick with tears when I recall the past, but I blink them back and swallow past the emotion that's clogged in my throat. I shouldn't cry. Tonight is about fun. It's about new beginnings, and I need to get out of my head and live in the present.

"Always, cupcake," I tease, calling her the nickname I gave her the night we gorged ourselves on red velvet cupcakes and cherry soda. It may sound like a gross combination, but at sixteen, we were all for it.

"Now hurry! Or I'll be dragging you out in your underwear." She laughs, flopping on my bed, leaving me to tug out the clothes that I've been mulling over for hours. Rukaiya loves to pick out clothes for me, and her choice for me tonight is nothing short of what I would call slutty.

Maybe I'm overexaggerating, but the pink dress that's hanging against the closet door doesn't leave much to the imagination. The black one, on the other hand, would more than likely be my pick.

The thin straps are cute, the neckline isn't too low, and the hemline hits mid-thigh. Scanning the shoe selection, I pick out a silver heeled sandal, which straps around my ankle and over my foot in a twisted figure-eight pattern.

Once I'm dressed, I make my way out to the spacious living room with Rukaiya hot on my heels. My gran is in the kitchen; I can hear the clinking of a mug, the whistle of the kettle, and soon, she enters.

"You look beautiful," Gran smiles when she takes in my outfit. "Where is this party again?" She asks as she settles in her armchair, which is located beside the large bay window.

"Some house on the hill," Rukaiya tells

her.

My gran's eyes meet mine, a flicker of something dancing in them before it's gone.

"Be careful, will you?"

"Always," I tell her as I press a kiss to her wrinkled cheek. Rukaiya and I make our way out the door, shutting it behind us before I stop on the wraparound porch.

"I'm not sure about this?" I glance down, taking in the dress once more. The material swishes against my thighs, the hemline is a little shorter than I anticipated, and I know if I were to bend over, there would be much more for people to see than just my tan lines from my running shorts.

"That," Rukaiya points with a smile on her pretty face, "is perfect." She slowly circles me, taking in every inch of me and my outfit. "We are going to wow all those college boys, and they'll be falling over themselves to get a taste of the new students—namely, us."

"You sound far too confident," I tell her with a nervous giggle. I should've worn jeans. They would've been much more comfortable.

"Of course, I am, because I know my *sugar cube* is a babe," she winks. As I follow her down the steps that take us out onto the main road, Rukaiya heads to the small blue BMW Coupe, which sits against the sidewalk, waiting for us.

Rukaiya's dad bought her a car for her seventeenth birthday. Even though she's not eighteen yet, she drives better than most adults I know.

This is nothing more than a one-horse town, and it intrigues me that there's a fancy high school and university that take up most of the Tynewood in both land and view. There are also some of the most beautiful homes that are accessible from the stunning tree-lined streets that I've ever seen in this forgotten corner of the country.

I pull open the passenger door and slip into the luxurious leather seat. Once I'm shut inside, I turn on the stereo, and Halsey's voice comes through the speakers as she sings 'Without Me.'

"Oh my god! This song." Rukaiya squeals,

turning up the volume, causing the bass to thrum through me. She weaves through the quiet street as we both sing along, and I find the tension in my muscles easing as we pass crowds of young people walking toward the large mansion that sits on the grassy hill where the party is meant to be taking place tonight. It reminds me of a castle where the owners would look over their subjects while sipping expensive drinks.

I had second thoughts about coming to this, even when Tarian asked, I wanted to refuse. But I remembered the old me sitting in my bedroom when all the parties at school were happening—the lonely girl who never really did anything fun. I promised to *not* be *her* when I got here.

Even though Tarian hasn't told us if this is his home or not, I can't help but be in awe of the beautiful house sitting atop the dark hill. A cold shiver runs down my spine at the shadows that dance along the garden as we near the entrance.

"Whose house is it?" I question Rukaiya

as she pulls up the long driveway, which has yellow flame-shaped lamps along the path, leading up to the house.

"Don't know, they said it's the Lancasters or something like that, but I could be wrong. I didn't take much notice of it." Her words filter into my mind, but I don't listen as she pulls to a stop.

What has my attention is the balcony on the second floor. There's a man, or boy, I can't tell in the dimly lit area, who is standing on a chair with a glass filled with liquid balancing on his forehead.

"Go, go, go!" I finally hear his friends chant when I exit the vehicle, my gaze pinned on the guy on the chair. He's dressed in dark clothes, jeans, I think, and a T-shirt that's riding up as he leans back, offering a flash of pale skin.

The chair is pulled out from under him, making me gasp and stepping forward as if I can help him from where I'm standing. But the moment the chair moves, he leaps up, the glass flying straight into the air, and I hold my breath to watch him land with ease on his feet.

He straightens as the glass tips and lands in his hand. The crowd erupts wildly, shouting and whistling. And I let out the whoosh of breath that I'd had locked in my lungs.

"He looks like a douche," Rukaiya mutters under her breath, before tugging me along. Before he disappears from sight, his gaze meets mine, and he winks, causing my stomach to flip flop wildly.

I don't know who he is, but all I can assume is that he's bad news and I most definitely need to stay away from him.

SEVEN

Ares

"You're a fucking legend," some guy tells me, and I nod, passing him without so much as a thank you. I know I'm a legend. I've been one since I was born, actually, before I was born. Making my way through the house, I saunter into the living room, which is filled with pretty girls in outfits that show off more than they hide.

"Hi, Ares," Kelli's voice comes from behind me, and I turn around to find her and her bitch squad smiling at me as if I were the prey. *Wrong, darling, I'm the fucking predator.*

"What are you doing here?" I question, not bothering with pleasantries because I know who invited her, and the moment I get my hands on him, he's going to fucking die.

"Party." She waves her hand around her as if she belongs in my fucking house. That's where she's wrong. If anything, Kelli should be shining my shoes and waiting on me hand and foot. After I caught her fucking some guy from school, I kicked her out of my bed and my house.

"A party that was invitation-only," I inform her, stalking through the clique she hangs out with. When I find my older brother, I pin him with a glare. "What the fuck is she doing here?" I glare at my brother, but his attention is caught by something behind me, and I know she followed me to the dining room where my brother is currently grinning stupidly at a girl I don't know.

"She's a student, her dad is a fucking Crown, Ares. You know this," he tells me, but there's a hint of a smirk that only irritates me further. He's such an asshole. I'd love to deck him in the jaw, watch him go down, and walk out of this fucking house. But he knows I can't. I'm meant to behave.

He turns away from me, pulling a blonde

onto his lap as he settles on the couch our folks bought on their last trip to Italy. The white leather is a pain in the ass to keep clean, and I'm certain, after tonight, it will be curbside or heading to a charity store.

"Get the fuck out," I spin on my heel and glare at Kelli who's now pouting at both brothers ignoring her. It's been years since I've wanted to fuck her, and having her here is nothing more than an annoyance.

"If you want me to leave, you'll have to throw me out yourself," she bites back, and I'm about to do just that when my gaze lands on someone behind her. The girl staring directly at me captures me more than Kelli ever did. Her gaze darts away, and her cheeks pink. *Well, hello there.* I think before looking at Kelli again.

"Suit yourself." Smirking, I saunter by her causing her to huff in frustration. She thought she'd get a rise out of me, and normally, she would've, but this time, I have a new distraction to introduce myself to.

When I reach her, I notice her hands are

twined around each other. Her fingers tremble as she glances around, not really looking at me. But the moment I step foot in front of her, those wide blue eyes meet mine.

"You're new," I tell her. Clearly, I'm off my game, stating the obvious. But being close to Dahlia isn't as easy as I thought it would be as her perfume wafts my way.

She smiles, nods, and murmurs, "Well done. You're very perceptive." Her body is encased in soft, silky material I'd love to rip off. Perhaps she'll allow me to do just that after I've gotten to know more about her. Tonight, I have my challenge set before me, and it's to see what this beauty has beneath her black dress.

"How about I show you around?"

"Oh, it's okay. I'm with a friend." She waves her hand in the air, but I don't see anyone else around her. She turns to look behind her and notices her so-called friend is nowhere to be seen.

"It seems she might have forgotten you're here," I remark, arching a brow when she glances back my way.

Her eyes remind me of a gemstone, the blue glinting in the lights coming from my mother's fancy chandeliers. I wonder just how pretty those blues would shimmer with lust burning in them.

"I-I guess she's found something to distract her," she tells me. "You're the guy who did that glass trick." This time, she lifts her hand to clamp it over her mouth when she recognizes me from earlier.

I saw her watching me. I knew I had to speak to her, and now that I'm inches from her, I want more. The moment the thought crosses my mind, some drunk asshole bumps into her, causing her slender frame to slam into mine.

Instinctively, my arms shoot out to steady her, practically picking her up and placing her behind me. I grab the asshole who looks far too young to even be in college and drag him to the door.

I can feel her behind me, following me to the circular driveway, she watches as I launch him onto the cobbled stones. A grunt falls from him, his gaze lifting up to meet mine as I peer down at him.

"Hey man, what's your beef?" He swipes his hands over his jeans as he pushes up to stand in front of me.

"This is my fucking house, and if I feel you've had enough, it's time for you to leave," I bite out. The gasp that sounds behind me makes my jeans feel tighter, and I can't wait to hear more of those sounds fall from her plump, glossy lips.

Once the asshole is booted, I turn to the little flower who's captured my attention. She's stunning. I shouldn't be so entranced by her, but I can't stop my roving appraisal. Her long dark hair hangs to the middle of her back, and those wide circles of cerulean turn my blood hot and my body rigid.

I reach for her chin with my thumb and forefinger, tilting her head back, so she's looking directly at me before I question, "Are you okay?"

She smiles, her cheeks tinting with a hint of a blush, and I'm thankful for the darkness shrouding us or she'd notice my growing bulge, which is ready to fuck her into next week.

"Thank you," she finally voices her words, and I'm enraptured by her sweetness. Even though she comes across as sweet and innocent, I wonder if there's more to this beauty than meets the eye.

"Ares." My best friend grips my shoulder, tugging me toward him. "Three girls ready for a group session," he informs me, and I can't help glancing at the beauty before me. She's blushing a deeper red than before.

"I'm busy man, you take it," I tell him, which only makes my best friend grin like an idiot.

"Did I ever tell you that you're the best fucking friend in the world?" He chuckles, slapping me on the back in camaraderie. I want to agree, but my gaze meets the wide eyes before me.

"So, tell me who you are?" I question, leaning in close. I offer her my hand, which for some unknown fucking reason, she accepts, and I pull her into a darkened corner of the staircase.

"I'm Dahlia," she informs me, tipping her chin with indignation, which makes me even more curious about the beauty. "And I don't fall for stupid games like yours," she bites out as if I planned that little interlude between my best friend and me. If only she knew that she will indeed fall right into the web I've set for her.

"Games? Oh, darling." I smirk. "I don't need to play games with girls. They want me because I'm a Lancaster."

Placing a hand on the wall behind her, I lean in closer before she places her palm on my chest, which burns me.

"Like I said, no games. Doesn't matter if it's your friend or you," she fires back, and I grip my chest in fake agony.

Does this beauty really think I'm letting her go after this display of perfect sass?

"I wasn't playing games, and like I said, sweetheart, I don't need to play games to get girls to spread their legs for me," I inform her as I stare down at the pretty little flower. I don't notice the slap that comes before it stings my face. "Jesus."

"Like I said, I don't deal well with *overconfident assholes*," she retorts before leaving me staring after her and the way she sways those luscious hips as she exits my house.

EIGHT
Dahlia

WHEN I OPEN MY EYES, I FIND MY GRAN STARING down at me, causing me to squeal as I scoot up in bed. Her face is tight with anxiety as she sits on the mattress.

"I heard you met Ares Lancaster," she tells me.

"What?" My sleep riddled mind plays catch up as my brows furrow in response to her random comment. "Yeah, he's—"

"Dangerous," she tells me. "Stay away from him." Her words are like ice water, causing me to shiver at the tone of her voice.

"What do you mean?"

"The Lancasters, the Durands, and the Calverts," she continues. "The three most prominent families in Tynewood."

"I don't understand. Tarian was friendly when I met him, and Etienne and Ares haven't given me any reason to be wary."

"Etienne Durand and Tarian Calvert are the other two boys, along with Philipe Lancaster," she speaks in a hushed whisper. "Stay out of their way, Dahlia."

"We all go to school together, Gran, it's not like I can hide from them," I tell her. Confusion settles in my mind, reminding me that I'm probably in more trouble with Ares than I thought. "What's so dangerous about them?" I should tell her about my confrontation with him. I should also tell her about what he said, but I find myself silent in both instances.

"I love you, Dahlia," she responds. "Just… be careful." I watch as she rises and heads to the door. She stops on the threshold, glancing at me from over her shoulder. "Don't get in their way. Study, focus on school, that's all you have to do."

With that, she leaves me alone in my bedroom more confused than I was before. There must be some explanation for this, for her warning, and I'm going to find out.

"Hey, cupcake," Rukaiya says in a soft, yet playful tone as she steps up beside me the moment I'm out of my car. She's dressed to kill in a pair of skinny jeans and a soft pink sheer top, which shows off the tight white tank underneath.

"Hey." Smiling over at my best friend, I ask, "Did you have fun last night?" She stayed at the party, I'm sure of it, or that dark ring under her eyes wouldn't be there.

"I did. I spent most of it talking to Tarian Calvert, he's so gorgeous," she gushes, and the name sends a spark of awareness through me. It's one of the names my gran warned me against.

I'm about to respond when Rukaiya's attention is dragged from me to something in the distance. When I follow her gaze, I see it. Three rogue kings stalking through the quad.

I recognize Ares, Tarian, and Etienne—their

clothes, their swagger, and those mischievous smirks. Only Tarian offers a smile. The silver glint of his lip piercing shines in the glow as he sucks in the corner of his mouth. The ring sits in the center of his lip.

He's dressed in a pair of dark jeans and a black T-shirt, which has a band name on it. Also, his feet are incased in a pair of black and white Chucks, and between his full lips is a lit cigarette.

"It's them," Rukaiya hisses in my ear as she leans in closer as if he'll hear her from this distance. The three of them stalk toward us, their focus zeroed in on me, and I wonder why I'm in their sights.

Perhaps it has something to do with Dad. Surely, if gran knows them, they should know the Miltons. Maybe now is my chance to speak to Ares. I'll have to get him alone, though I don't want this to go any further than it needs to.

They reach us, causing all eyes to fall on us. The whole student body is alert as if they're gods, and we're mere mortals. Ares' dark gaze locks on mine as his mouth kicks into a grin.

"The little flower," he coos, his words practically drip with disdain and something else—lust? I don't know, I can't place it, but I step up to him, our bodies almost flush with each other, even though I'm nearly a head shorter than him.

"We need to talk," I bite out, ignoring his glare.

"Ooh, Ares is in trouble." This comes from Etienne; he seems to be the more playful one.

"Shut it, lover boy," Ares growls, gripping my bicep with his large hand and dragging me away from the group. Once we're alone, he shoves me against a tree, and I can feel everyone's watchful eyes on what's happening between us.

He leans in, his mouth inches from mine, and I wonder if he's going to kiss me, but he doesn't. As if he changes his mind quickly, he allows his lips to trail over the shell of my ear.

"What is it that you'd like to say to me, flower?" he murmurs, causing goosebumps to dot my skin. Even though I'm fully clothed, his voice makes me feel as if I'm naked.

"My father," I start, wondering if I'll anger him, but also, not caring if I do because this needs to be sorted out.

Ares steps back, his hands fisting at his sides, but his darkened, angry stare pierces me as if he's attempting to hurt me with the thoughts in his mind. There's danger in his eyes, and if he could kill me with it, I'm sure I'd be lying at his feet. I watch his body shake for a moment before he breathes the tension away, and soon enough, he's relaxed.

He tips his head to the side, regarding me through narrowed slits, with dark lashes fluttering over smooth, alabaster cheeks. "What about him?"

"You know him." It's not a question, but he nods anyway. "Look, he's dead."

"I know he is," he tells me with a satisfied grin, which makes me shudder, "and he deserved what he got. So will you for coming here."

"I have nowhere else to go." My words are filled with disdain. "Why do you hate me?

If you had beef with my dad, it's over; he's dead."

"He may be dead," Ares says, stepping up against me once more. The bark of the tree pressing into my back. "But his bloodline,"— he trails his knuckles over my cheek and down to my throat, and his gaze drops to where my pulse point is rioting— "lives on in you."

I cross my arms in front of my chest, which causes his eyes to lower briefly to my breasts before snapping back to mine. At least it puts some distance between us because I can't think straight with him so close.

"Whatever happened is in the past. I've said it's done, so it's done. I'm not running away from this town because some asshole with a god complex tells me to," I bite out, shoving him backward, which earns me a gasp from our audience who I'd long ago forgotten about.

"You know, Dahlia," Ares smirks. "If you weren't my toy to play with, I'd probably fuck you. No girl has had the balls to fight back before, and I quite like it."

"Fuck you, Ares Lancaster." My words earn me silence this time. Nobody moves. It's as if we're the only animated people here because Ares and I are the only ones who seem to be breathing.

Even Etienne and Tarian are still as statues. The shrill ringing of a bell from somewhere on campus sounds and Ares' head snaps in that direction, before offering me one final glare.

He moves beside me, stopping right at my shoulder before he tells me. "This isn't over. I like it rough. I like it when you fight me. Perhaps I may even find out if the good cop's daughter is still a sweet little virgin." With that, he leaves me staring at nothing. I'm rigid with frustration. Every inch of me is filled with tension; yet, my hands are trembling.

"What the hell was that?" Rukaiya's voice breaks the trance I'm in, but it's as if Ares has magical powers that keep me grounded, I feel like I can't move my feet. His words weren't an empty threat. I have a feeling that when Ares says he's going to do something he doesn't back down.

And I might be crazy, but right down in my gut, everything clenches at the thought of Ares touching me in places I haven't felt pleasure in a while. Maybe that's why my body is hot from the interaction, *it's been too long*.

"He's an asshole," I tell my best friend, and it's as if he can hear me because he turns to regard me once more. The other two guys flanking him both glance over their shoulders, too, and I swear on my life, I see their eyes glow with something supernatural. Shaking my head, I attempt to clear it of the crazy thoughts and look at my best friend. "Let's go to class."

NINE

Ares

T<small>HE MOMENT</small> I <small>STEP FOOT IN THE HOUSE</small>, I hear it. Fucking music blaring as if we're at a concert. I spent years wishing I could be like Philipe: go to concerts, meet bands, and live the party lifestyle. He's constantly heading out to different events, which bodes well for me because I get VIP tickets to all the events.

I hit the stairs to the first floor where his room is located and shove open his bedroom door. I'm met with the sight of my brother getting head from some blonde bimbo. She's so engrossed in her task that she doesn't notice me slump myself into the burgundy leather wingback chair at his desk.

His gaze meets mine, a smirk playing at his lips, and pleasure written all over his face. He grips her hair, fisting the long golden strands, and shoves his hips upward, causing her to gag and gurgle around him.

"Stop being a dick," I bite out, and the muffled scream that comes from his companion causes me to chuckle. He comes hard, with a groan of satisfaction that bounces around the room.

When he's done, he jerks away from her as if he were in a daze, and now, he's finally seeing her clearly. She shifts toward me, her blue eyes widen in shock, and I can't help but offer her a little wave, making her blush a bright red that would put apples to shame.

"Get out, we're done," Philipe tells her, zipping up his jeans.

"What?" Her face is a picture of shock and annoyance.

He rises, rounding the chair, and finds her purse lying on his bed. Tossing it toward her, he offers another smile. "I said, get out. We're done."

I watch the show, intrigued by my brother. Even though we're not that far apart in age, he's an asshole of note; whereas, I'm kinder to the girls I bring home. Sometimes.

"You're every bit the asshole they told me you would be," she throws back in an attempt to insult Philipe, leaning in to press her manicured fingernail to his chest.

"And you're every bit the cock hungry whore I heard you were. Now, unless you're going to suck my brother's dick, I suggest you get out," he taunts. Ignoring her fury, he turns and heads to his desk. I watch the blonde huff from his bedroom, slamming the door so loudly, I wonder how it hasn't come off its hinges.

"Well, that was entertaining," I chuckle. "You should come home more often. It's not every day I see a girl running from the house in tears."

"Like you don't break any hearts," he tells me as he glances over his shoulder at me, and I shrug in response since he's right. "So, how was Dahlia's introduction to the Sovereign? Did you take her to the church?"

"I haven't taken her to the church yet, but

she knows something is up. We saw her at school again today, made introductions. She's a feisty one."

"And that makes your dick hard." It's not a question, so I don't offer a response, but he's not wrong. I loved the way she fought back. "Take her to the church, find out more, we need as much information about her as we can get. I reckon that the grandmother of hers has been spewing lies."

"She's definitely not scared of us... yet."

"You think?" He arches a brow, settling in the chair opposite me with a cigarette hanging from between his lips. A flick of the lighter burns cherry red, and soon, there's a scent of smoke wafting in the air.

"Dad will kill you if he knew you were smoking in here," I tell him.

Philipe shrugs nonchalantly. He's always just done whatever he wants. I'm not shocked, but when he turns to me, he tugs off his shirt, showing me the dark ink on his left pectoral. The crown that sits there forces me to my feet, and I'm inches from him.

Our crest looks good with the shield, which has GS in the center and the year the society was formed, 1854. Beneath the Gilded Sovereign crest is the society's motto, 'Protect the weak, avenge the broken,' and it's perfectly centered to the icon of my legacy.

"This is new," I remark, noting the ink healing on his tanned skin.

"Just over an hour ago," he affirms, pulling in a deep drag from the cigarette. The white plume of smoke that tumbles from his mouth envelops us both, and for a moment, I relax in the smell. "I waited three years longer than I should have."

His voice is filled with contempt. I know why, his inking had to happen years ago, but with our mother being murdered, Philipe only stepped into his rightful place two months ago.

"I want this, bro," I tell him, stepping back to regard my brother. "I want this more than anything."

"More than the girl?" He quirks a brow as he sucks on the cigarette. There's a knowing glint in his eye.

"You seem to forget what her family did to ours. I'm not one to dip my dick in liars," I tell him, shrugging off his inquisitive glare. He clucks his tongue at me, and I know he can read through the bullshit.

Philipe chuckles as he regards me. "Brother, you've had a few bitches in your bed, Kelli come to mind?" His brow arches and I have to give him that. My choices haven't always been good, I'll be the first to admit it. "Besides, there aren't any rules against getting pleasure out of a job." His voice is cold, reminding me more of our father than ever before.

Philipe was Dad's favorite. The eldest son, the one who would take over the society from him. We grew up knowing I was a mistake, and that made me try to prove myself to them more times than I can count.

Living in the shadow of a sibling is shitty.

But it also makes you work harder, it makes you focus on your goals.

And that's what I'm doing right now.

I meet familiar green eyes and nod.

"Perhaps I should play this differently. But I want more information about her before I start."

He nods with a smile. "I have a folder for you. Once you're inked, you'll have access to everything else in the vault. The other elders will bè there, don't fuck this up." There's a warning in his tone, one that makes me antsy.

"I have to go, but... tomorrow night, when I get that tattoo on my chest, the only way anyone is taking it from me is to cut it off." I turn to leave, stopping at his door, and I glance over my shoulder at my brother. His light brown hair shimmers under the lamps that hang low from the ceiling. His room is dark with the old furniture that is better suited to an old castle. His four-poster bed is made of old mahogany wood, and the desk matches it, with shadows that play over the space.

A painting hangs above a fireplace, the image of our great grandfather slaughtering men on a battlefield stares down at the room. I wonder how my brother ever brought girls back here; surely, they'd be frightened out of their minds. But then again, my brother is a lady's man. He can get any chick to drop her panties in five seconds flat.

I step out into the hallway and head to my bedroom. The moment I'm in the sanctuary, I shut the door, taking note of how different the room is compared to Philipe's.

My bed is made of a metal frame, with an almost cage-like structure beneath it. I like to play with my pets when I have them here. Women like to be manhandled, they enjoy giving up power, and I enjoy taking it.

Perhaps Philipe is right, I can get some pleasure from the little flower before I snip her stem for good. Flopping on my bed, I stare up at the ceiling as I smile, thinking about how good it will feel to hold a life in my hands.

I'm coming for you, Dahlia.

TEN

Dahlia

Every interaction I've had with Ares has been on a loop in my mind, and I hate the asshole. He's everything I don't like—overconfident, snarky, and pompous. But I can't deny he's hot. There's a magnetism to him that pulls me in, and each time I recall our interaction, my stomach is in knots.

Pushing open the car door, I step out of the vehicle, taking in the campus. Yesterday, I didn't fully take in how stunning it is. Mainly because Rukaiya couldn't stop talking as we walked up to the main entrance. Only a few days have passed, but it's starting to feel like home.

Everything is so different from the city. It feels as if this town is haunted by its ancestors, the founders of this small piece of the country still watching over those who've come after. The main building is a looming structure of red brick with church-like steeples made of what looks like onyx metal.

The carvings are so lifelike and intricate, I'm left speechless as I stare up at them. There are four other buildings on the land, which make up the whole university. Smiling, I grab my backpack and shut the car door, making my way up the paved pathway.

My dad grew up here. He told me about the town once or twice, but he never went into great detail about his friends, or even if he kept in touch with anyone here. Now, I'll never be able to speak to him again. Sadness hits me hard in the chest, so much so that I have to bite the inside of my cheek to keep from crying.

If Gran knows the founding families, perhaps my dad has some old friends here. Maybe I can learn more about him. Even growing up with him, he was almost like a stranger to me. There were never any photos from his youth; I didn't even realize my gran was still alive until she came to D.C. to collect me.

My father died, and I couldn't even have a funeral because there wasn't a body. That's what Fergus told me. My father's partner and the man who joined him on dangerous missions. I wonder what he would've done if he were here now.

I miss my dad and his overprotectiveness, but I'm here, and I'm excited to start a new life and focus on my future. All my life, my dad had people watching over me, especially when he was on a job. I would live at one of the safe houses, or he'd have one of the detectives *babysit* me. Although he's gone, I think deep down, he's still got eyes on me. I wouldn't put it past him.

A squeal catches my attention, and I glance over at a group of college students laughing and chatting, some sitting on the benches at the lunch table and other's surrounding it: jocks and their groupies.

Some things don't change. No matter how old you get. There are always cliques that seem to gather together.

"Hi." A stunning brunette strolls up to me with a broad smile on her face. "I'm Grecia." Her hand shoots out, and I capture it and shake it.

"I'm Dahlia," I tell her.

"Welcome to Tynewood. I'm the president of the sorority—"

"Oh, I don't know if—"

"Why don't you come by tonight," she says, handing me a flyer. "Before you decide, listen to what we do, and perhaps, we can change your mind?" With a wink, she strolls off and makes a beeline for the group of girls who are heading toward their classes.

I scan the flyer, noting the house number which I recall seeing when I drove up to school the first day. Even though it could be good to meet new people, I already know this is something that would have my anxiety ripping a hole in my chest.

Shoving the page into my purse, I make my way toward the steps when Rukaiya comes bounding up to me. She must be feeling better.

"What happened between you and the hottie? I need to know if you got lucky or if I'm going to need to find you someone else," Rukaiya teases, a smile wide on her pretty face. I've had two boyfriends in school, but neither of them was serious. Not that we could be since dear old dad wouldn't let me out of his sight alone with a boy.

"I had a little run-in with the asshole who lives in that house before I left the party," I tell her, hugging my books closer to me. The jumper I'm wearing is far too warm for the sunny day, and my jeans feel as if they've been painted on. I'm nervous talking about him. For some reason, I feel as if he's coming for me. Like he's going to appear out of nowhere and act like a goddamn asshole again.

"Oh. My. God. What happened?" She's excitedly bouncing on the balls of her feet, her eyes wide with shock, and I realize I'm going to have to give her something, or she'll never stop hounding me about it.

"All I'm saying is Ares Lancaster is an asshole; he's overconfident, rude, and—"

"Particularly handsome," the deep drawl from behind me interrupts my tirade, causing my heart to catapult into my throat.

Pivoting on my heel, I find those same hazel eyes from last night staring at me. The corner of his mouth has curled into a mischievous smirk, and I can't deny he looks even better in the daylight. But he's bad news, and I need to steer clear of him.

"And my day has just plummeted into hell," I utter, turning around, I stalk toward the large campus that sits in front of me. I leave my best friend to deal with Ares. I'm not so lucky, though, because he follows me; his hand reaches out and grabs my arm, preventing me from getting away.

"Hell is so far from where you are right now, darlin'. Can we not do this bullshit?" he questions, waving his free hand in the air between us.

"Do what *bullshit* exactly?" I question, pulling free from his hold.

He runs his fingers through his wavy dark hair, causing the strands to point in all directions, which only makes him look more alluring than I'd care to admit. He's far too handsome for his own good. When he meets my gaze, I note the flecks of green in his irises; they glint like shimmering jewels when the sun hits them just right.

Shrugging his broad shoulders, he offers me one more grin before responding, "I'm not the asshole you think I am." He shoves his hands into his jean pockets, lowering is head, so he can peek at me through those thick black lashes.

"Oh? And your display last night wasn't you trying to get into my pants?" I question, arching a brow at him. I cross my arms in front of me, folding in on myself, causing those gem-like eyes to dart toward my breasts.

The low chuckle that vibrates through his chest makes my heart flip, and my stomach flutters nervously when he steps closer to me. The air is thick with the scent of his cologne— mint, and sandalwood—and it's intoxicating.

"I never said I don't want to get into your pants, pretty girl," he tells me in a hushed tone. "I just said I'm not an asshole. Let me take you out?"

"Hi, Ares," a dark-haired girl steps up beside him, practically climbing up his body. He's tall, probably just over six feet, broad-shouldered with strong, muscled thighs, and this petite little thing could easily crawl up his leg like a kitten wanting attention.

"What the fuck do you want, Kelli?" he bites out, his eyes flashing a darker shade of caramel as he turns to look at her.

"Just saying hi." She smiles sweetly, then pins me with a glare that's meant to have me stepping back, but I've dealt with bullies all my life, and this is nothing compared to what I've been through. Jealousy burns in her gaze, which doesn't faze me. "Who's this?"

"This, is leaving," I utter, before making my exit from what is turning into an impossible situation. I knew Ares would be trouble, and I want no part of it.

I'm far from Ares and his groupie by the time I allow myself to inhale a calm breath. I don't do drama, and girls like that, are more trouble than I'd like to put up with.

I'm up the steps and near the entrance when I find Rukaiya again.

"What happened there?" she asks, arching a perfectly sculpted eyebrow at me.

"He has some chick crawling all over him. I don't want this bullshit, all I need is to study and graduate. That's my focus for the next four years," I tell her.

"He's hot, though," she murmurs conspiratorially with a giggle, and I can't deny she's right. He is hot, he's every girl's perfect guy, but that's the problem. Every girl here wants him, and he's likely had most of the girls on campus.

We head into our first class of the day, which is History. I've always had a fascination with this subject—since I was a kid—and soon, I'll get to list it as one of my majors.

"Everyone take a seat." The man at the front of the class is not Professor Harding, who we had a few days ago and I wonder where he is. The man before us is dressed in a pair of black slacks and a white button-up shirt.

He doesn't look like the teachers I envisioned who would be here or the ones back in D.C. at my old school. His dark hair has a smattering of gray giving him a salt and pepper head of hair, which tells me he's much older than we are.

Brown eyes, framed with black-rimmed spectacles, glance around the room. Based on how he looks, I'd put him at about mid-forties.

Rukaiya and I find a seat in the back of the class, and I pull out my notebook and pen. Before the doors close, my heart leaps into my throat when Ares saunters into the classroom and greets the man at the front as if they're friends.

As soon as the teacher faces us, I see it. They're related. They have to be. Both have those luminous eyes that seem to look right through me. The same jawline adorns both men, and there's a hint of mischievousness that is clear in their smiles.

"Is that his dad?" Rukaiya hisses under her breath at me.

Shrugging, I whisper, "I don't know."

"Good morning minions, I'm Mr. Lancaster, I'm standing in for Professor Harding for the next couple of weeks. Lucky you," he smirks, as he says this, his voice taking on a note of sarcasm, but it's his name that causes my heart to slam against my ribs. "I'm here out of courtesy, so I'd appreciate your utmost attention. I don't take kindly to talking in class, and I certainly don't tolerate tardiness."

Silence fills the room, and there's a heaviness in the air. Mr. Lancaster turns his gaze on each of us as if he can pick out all those who are troublemakers, and those who are studious.

"Will you tell us about the history of Guild Hall and the Sovereign?" One of the students in front of the class questions, his hand in the air.

Mr. Lancaster clears his throat, his hand in front of his mouth, hiding what I can only guess is a smile because the corners of his eyes crinkle. "Those are fairytales, but if you're good little boys and girls, I may tell you."

His gaze roves over the class as if he's mentally checking each of our names off a list. But it's his expression that only seems to confirm my suspicions that he has to be Ares' father. And I'm proven correct in my assumption when he continues.

"My name is Abner Lancaster, this school, the house on the hill where most of you partied last night, is my legacy." He offers a quick glance at Ares, and I'm sure he isn't happy about finding his house in tatters this morning.

He turns toward the blackboard, picking up a piece of chalk. He writes down the name of the school along with his name. While his back is turned, I take him in, broad shoulders and torso, which taper down into narrowed hips. His black slacks are tight around his ass and thighs, and I can't stop myself from staring. For an older man, there's something magnetic about him.

"He's hot," Rukaiya whispers again, her words making my cheeks heat as he turns at that second and pins us with a sharp glare.

"Is there something you'd like to tell the class, miss..." he watches my best friend, waiting for her to respond.

"It's Miss Harrison," she sasses, "and I was just telling my friend, Miss Milton, over here, how excited I am to be in your class, Sir." The blatant lie has Abner narrowing his gaze at her as if reading all her dirty thoughts about him. Because, if I know my best friend, there are some sordid images in her head right now. For a moment, I wonder if he's going to call her out as silence hangs in the air around us.

"Thank you," he finally responds, then turns toward the projection system, which he flicks on. The bright light shines on the white wall beside the board, and he turns to Ares. "Lights."

Once the classroom has been drenched in darkness, an image appears on the wall, a photo of the house we were in last night. But this was taken a long time ago if the sepia tone is anything to go by.

"You wanted a history lesson on the school," Abner says, "well sit back. For our first lesson, I'll take it easy on you. Tomorrow, if I'm in a good mood, I might give you a pop quiz." He informs us with a satisfied smile, and I have to admit, he is handsome. I can see where Ares gets his looks from.

My gaze flits to the younger man in question who I find watching me intently. He doesn't look away when our gazes lock, and I hold his for a moment before turning my attention to the photo in an attempt to focus, even though I know it's futile. When Ares is around, nothing makes sense. Least of all my stupid fluttering heartbeat.

This is going to be a very long four years of my life.

ELEVEN

Ares

I watch my father shuffle papers on the desk. He doesn't look at me, because when he did the roll call in class, she offered up her name. Her last name stuck out at me, slapping me across the face.

"I want the go ahead to deal with the girl."

My father glares at me from his seat where he's marking papers. His gaze burning with frustration at me, but I don't care. This is something I need. Surely, he can understand that.

"Dad, she's right here, I can do anything to toy with her. She's in *my* town," I utter in frustration as he just looks at me without response.

It takes far too long for him to think

about it before he finally tells me, "I know it's Patrick's daughter, but we need to be careful."

"Tell me you'll allow me free reign?" My question stills him for a moment. He has to at least consider this. I begged him to allow me to get my revenge the moment I became one of the Sovereign, and now I have the daughter of the man I wanted to kill right here in Tynewood.

"Let me think about it, Ares." He doesn't look convinced. As if he wants to refuse my request. If this were Philipe, there would be no question.

"Is this because I'm volatile?"

Father sighs, shaking his head before responding. "Let me talk to the Crowns, and we'll decide what the best course of action is." My dad, one of the Sovereign Elders. Even though I'm second born, I am a crown as my father's the head of the society and his colleague, Leonard Harding. His daughter, Kelli Harding, isn't allowed to become one of the Crowns.

Two Lancasters have never sat at the table

before. The vote came in only a month ago for me to be there, and I'm still coming to terms with it.

All my life I'd grown up knowing Philipe, my older brother, would be at that coveted table, but now, we're both named as successors.

"I want her, I want to break her. She should never have come here," I insist once more, but he doesn't look at me. Not yet. When he does pin me with a glare, I know he'll refuse. "The Sovereign wouldn't refuse me a job like this," I tell him. "They're all too old to do anything themselves." I can't help smiling when I say it, earning me a chuckle from the old man.

I shouldn't mock them because I want this. I hunger to show them what I'm made of, that I belong at the table alongside my brother and the other new leaders who will soon take over. I was named after one of the gods, so I should, in fact, be right there, wearing my crown.

"Ares," Dad sighs as he sets his pen down and meets my gaze, "I doubt she's here without eyes on her. Fergus Harrison is her father's best friend and partner. He's moved here without any need to. Granted, we've got a background check on him, but other than that, we don't know what his ulterior motive is."

"I can always put pressure on him. Find out what he's doing here."

"No, we wait. You're too impulsive, Ares. You'll start a war."

"And you didn't?" I bite out in frustration. This isn't new, it's an ongoing feud that came to a head five years ago, and I'm done waiting. "Listen to me, Dad," I lean in, placing my palms on his desk. "If I can sit at the table you ruled over, if I can be one of the Sovereign, then they can gift me this as my first task. I'm ready."

"Let me speak to the others," he tells me earnestly. "We don't like eyes on us, and you're far too impulsive right now. If you can keep calm, do this without anyone finding out, or even a hint of a rumor about us, I'll allow it."

"What if I start the rumors?"

He pierces me with a glare. "Is this about revenge? Or is it about the girl?" he asks.

I shrug, not knowing how to answer him because I don't know why she's gotten under my skin. When I saw her talking to Tarian, my blood heated to the point of pain. I wanted to punch my best friend in the gut. Now that I have Dad's blessing, I will make her run so far, so fast, she'll never come back to my town. Perhaps it's time for me to play a twisted little game.

"I like toying with my food."

Another low rumble vibrates through his chest, the corners of his eyes crinkle with amusement. "Playing with the prey isn't something I like to do because the more time you spend around her, the more you'll start to care," he tells me, something I refuse immediately by shaking my head.

"She's nothing to me," I bite out, crossing my arms in front of my chest, as I regard my father. "My anger and need for revenge outweigh my craving for her body."

He shakes his head as if he knows something I don't. But I don't let up. I've had girls before and shoved them out the door after. Love? It's a useless emotion that only causes pain. And if I were to fall for someone, it wouldn't be the poisonous little flower who's walked into my town.

"Fine. Break her... If you can," my father challenges. "We'll need to be careful, though, a warning would be best. But if she goes running to Fergus, I'll be forced to do something to shut her up myself."

"I'll make you proud," I affirm with a smirk.

He's about to respond when his cell phone jolts us both from the conversation. When he answers, I can't hear the caller's voice, but I don't move to give him privacy.

"Yes," he responds to a question I'm itching to hear. "I'll have the boys on it. I have a feeling Harrison is going to cause problems," he says again, then listens further with a few nods before hanging up. "It seems you boys have your first job." He cuts his gaze to mine.

"What?"

"Dahlia Milton is yours to do with as you wish. We have another visitor to town, and I want eyes on her. She came along with your toy. Rukaiya Harrison can be a task for either Etienne or Tarian. She may cause more disruptions than we anticipated." He doesn't seem to be perturbed, and I wonder why he's not angry.

"What happened to Patrick?" I ask, knowing the man is dead, but I have a feeling my father had something to do with his demise.

Dad doesn't respond, and I wonder why he decided to keep it from me. It's not like him to do something without the Sovereign knowing, so this has me on edge.

"Did you do something? Did you have him killed?" I question, glaring at him. My father is not someone you fuck around with. He can easily kill someone with a flick of his wrist, but right now, I don't give a shit.

"Be at the meeting tonight, we'll discuss your inking," he tells me, not responding to my question. He must've had Patrick killed. Tonight, I'll get the tattoo on my chest, right between the shoulder blades, the crest of our family, of the Sovereign. "You can go."

His dismissiveness makes me wary. My father doesn't do something because he wants to, he does it because it's all part of a larger plan. And I wonder just what Abner is hiding behind his calm exterior.

"I'll be there." I make my move to walk away and leave him to his work.

"Ares," Father calls to me when I reach the door, causing me to glance over my shoulder. "She's not your friend. Even if her father is dead, she's still a liability."

"I didn't think she was my friend." I grin. "And since you've done my job for me, I have nothing to worry about."

He shakes his head because he knows I'm angry with him. Even if he tells me not to do anything to the girl, he knows I'll disobey him. Normally, I wouldn't, but my anger always gets the better of me. And Dahlia has to pay for her father's sins.

She'll beg for mercy.

And I don't know a thing about offering it.

Sauntering down the quad, I take note of the large metal clock on the tower, which sits in the center of the grassy area where most of the students hang out during lunch.

The red brick structure is a part of my legacy that's still standing, and I can't help but be proud of it. Black metal makes up the circle and hands of the white-faced clock. Where the number twelve should be is our coat of arms. A shield with the ribbon beneath it and the date 1854 inscribed on it, the same year the Sovereign was founded.

"Yo, man." Etienne makes his way toward me over the freshly cut green grass. His eyes are hidden by shades, and he's dressed in his signature leather jacket, along with ripped black jeans. He's convinced he's god's gift to women, which is why we're mates. Because we play the good guy, bad guy all too often.

I bump knuckles with him before greeting, "What's up?"

"I see the new girl arrived," he tells me.

He knows about Dahlia and her father. He knows how much I hate the bastard, but he doesn't know how much I want to break the little flower.

"She's a problem," I tell him. "I was just talking to Dad, her father is dead, so she's here, living with the old lady." My admission causes a smirk to curl on his lips.

"And we're going to toy with her?" he questions, arching a brow at me. The thick, dark curve higher than his black sunglasses makes me chuckle. He's worse than a fucking woman with his perfect eyebrows.

"Is there any other way?" I respond, shrugging my shoulder. Just then, I notice the little spitfire walking toward the parking lot. Nudging my chin toward her, I tell him, "My father took the one thing I needed away from me; it's time I step up and show him I'm worthy of my crown."

"I'm right beside you, brother," he tells me with a hand on my shoulder, offering me a reassuring squeeze. I knew he would be; he's always been there, through our darkest moments and through the most fucked up scenarios.

Dahlia's friend comes running up beside her, and Etienne's whistle is loud when he takes in the girl in tight jeans that seem to be painted on her. He can have her; my gaze is locked on the little flower.

"My dick likes the blonde a whole lot," Etienne tells me with a chuckle. "What's the friend's name?"

"That would be Rukaiya, her father moved here with her, and Dad reckons something's fishy about the guy. He and Patrick Milton were partners." I push off the wall and make my way down the quad with my best friend hot on my heels. We reach them as they step off the grass and onto the gravel of the parking lot.

"Hey, baby," Etienne coos at the blonde while I keep my gaze locked on Dahlia. "Need a ride?" He offers, and I know he ain't talking about a goddamn lift home. He takes a step up to the best friend who seems more interested in her phone than his attempt at being a charming asshole. I have to bite back my laugh when she steps by him with a sassy wink.

No women can resist Etienne.

That's the reason we call him the god of love, well, lust more like. Because his real name is Eros Etienne Durand, but he's forbidden us from calling him by his first name.

"I have my own ride," blondie bites out, rolling her eyes as if he's annoying her. It's the first time I've ever seen my best friend not get a giggle and a blush from a girl.

I take in the dark-haired beauty, the one who I'm going to love to see bend and break. "You comin' to my party this weekend." It's not a question; it's a statement as I gesture toward the stoned faced little flower. Dahlia turns her head toward me, peering at me with her eyes narrowed, as if she's wary of me, and shrugs.

"Come on, being at a new school, you got to make friends somehow." I tip my head to the side in an attempt to read her reaction to me. A small tremble, nothing more than that, and it makes my work harder, so I get closer to her.

"I have school work," she tells me, shouldering her rucksack as if it's heavy.

"I'll see you there." I lean in, before whispering, "My place, seven-thirty." I pivot on my heel and walk away, leaving both girls staring after me. Etienne is beside me in an instant as I press the key fob of my sleek, onyx Audi Spyder. The darkened windows offer privacy, which comes in handy when I have one of the pretty freshmen sitting next to me.

"She's a tough nut," Etienne remarks as I peel out of the parking lot, with one last glance in the rear-view mirror at the girl who's becoming the focus of all my attention.

"Easy pickings, man," I tell him as I swerve through the cars and head up the hill toward the house. Lancaster Mansion is one of the biggest and most infamous properties in the town. Beside us is the Calvert mansion, and on the other side of Tynewood are the Durand's.

"I doubt she'll come to the party," he tells me.

Smiling, I cut a glance toward him before shaking my head. "You underestimate me, lover boy," I grin, earning me a punch on the shoulder. As I pull up to the house, I note my brother's blacked-out Lambo parked in the drive. He's nowhere to be seen, and I wonder who's bed he's in right now. One thing about my brother—he's worse than me when it comes to breaking hearts.

Being five years older, he's had a string of girls racing from the house on numerous occasions when he still lived at home. Me and the guys would be driving up to the house when we'd see some pretty girl in her car, mascara running down her cheeks, and Philipe grinning like he'd just won the goddamned lottery.

"What's he still doing here?" Etienne questions as he pushes open the door, stepping out and waiting for me.

"We have Sovereign meeting tonight," I tell him before exiting the car, rounding the front to meet him on the other side. He follows me into the foyer and down toward the back

131

of the house where the kitchen is located.

The moment I set foot in the large space, I find our chef, Monique, working on something at the cooker. She glances my way and smiles when I give her a wink. She and her mother have been working for my family since I can remember.

Monique is in her early thirties, pretty enough for an older lady. Even though I've had a quick thing with Mo, there's nothing more for me in her bed. It's how I've always been. One night is more than enough. But right now, not even the promise of the inking can distract me. My mind is still on the little flower.

"Mo," I greet her, before pulling open the fridge to grab two bottles of beer and handing one to Etienne.

"Dinner will be at six," she tells me. "Your dad called to make sure that you and your brother will be here."

"Yeah, sure," I responded noncommittally. He probably wants a nice family dinner before he tells us the moment Philipe is in charge, I'll be second chair. I leave her in the kitchen and make my way up to my bedroom with Etienne following. Once inside, I shut the door and turn on the stereo.

"So, what's the plan?" he asks, before taking a swig of his drink.

"You want the little blonde?"

He nods.

"Keep her busy," I suggest with a smirk because I know it's a job he'll enjoy. "I want to take her friend to the church and see just how quickly I can get her to leave town," I tell him, knowing I should've planned this better, but fuck it. That's the only place I can think of that will ensure she obeys my fucking rules.

"You sure you want her in there?"

I'm not sure I do. But where else can we toy with the guilty girl? Fuck it. I shrug, gulping down the bubbly liquid. My bedroom door opens, and Philipe stalks in, his eyes glance between Etienne and me before he shuts the door and tosses a small hard drive on the bed.

I tip my chin toward the device before asking, "What's that?"

133

"Check it out," he smirks, settling himself on the chair at my desk.

He's the inked god the girls make him out to be, but he doesn't show it off. His club is infamous in Los Angeles for the shit that goes down in the basement. I've never seen it myself, but I've heard whispers.

"Hey, Etienne," he greets. "You doing good?"

"Yeah," *lover boy* grins. "I guess you heard about our new project?"

"That's why I'm here."

I grab the small device and open my laptop, which I left on my bed this morning. Once it boots up, I push the small drive-in, clicking on the folder that appears, where I find photos of my new toy.

"Where'd you get these?" I ask my brother, glancing at him for my answer.

"She spent a month in L.A. when her father was meeting with the CEO of Garrick Tech. Some part-time stint that ended as quickly as it began," he tells me. "She's hot," Philipe says, and I nod in agreement.

The photos of her jogging don't calm the heat that makes my dick throb with need. A tiny sports bra, tight jogging bottoms, and her stomach bare is a sight I'll certainly be keeping in my spank bank for later on.

"She was in the city," I utter, cutting my gaze toward him. "Anything interesting we should know?"

"She met with Eric Burrell," he informs us. The name causes me to still. I wait for him to continue, which he does when he notices my expression. "I think she's been training. I don't know why. I mean her dad has every fucking bodyguard shadowing her."

"I didn't see any when she arrived at school. And no-one's watching her place down the way," I tell him.

"Dad called me earlier, told me you want this one. All I'm saying is, be careful. I doubt a fallen undercover cop will allow his daughter to live with an old lady and not have someone watching her. Fergus, her father's ex-partner lives here now," he says. "There's something off about this whole thing. I need you to watch your back." He should be the one to take this because he's the eldest, but Philipe moved out before shit hit the fan. He wasn't here when it happened. I can't even talk about that night.

"Yeah, I will," I affirm. "Do you think Fergus was in on that night?"

He shakes his head to my question, knowing precisely what night I'm talking about. We've never really spoken about it, but there's an underlying understanding.

"Don't worry about me, bro. I'm a big boy now, I can take care of myself."

My mind flits back instantly to the moment I smelled the metallic scent wafting through the air. I was the one who witnessed the bloody violence that took place that fateful night, and even if Philipe expressed his interest, I would fight him on it.

"Fine. But remember, this isn't going to be easy. You may have to do shit you're not comfortable with," he warns, causing me to chuckle.

"Me? Not comfortable? Brother, I don't think you know me very well."

He narrows his eyes regarding me before he nods. "I know my brother, and I know there are things I'd rather not have you do."

"Why? Because I'll feel guilty about it? Fuck guilt. I didn't see any in that asshole's eyes when he stole the most important part of our life, and Dad took that from me, now it's time for me to take what I need. This time, it's not just a job, it's war. A cruel war." I bite out as anger shudders through me. His nostrils flare when my words hit home. He knows as well as I do that Patrick killed our mother. Even though he wasn't home that night, he knows from the security footage. My only concern is why we had to wait so fucking long to do anything about it.

"Those who are responsible will pay." He's trying to assure me. "One way or another."

"Yeah, my fucking way," I vow through clenched teeth. Shoving the laptop away, I pick up my drink and down my beer in a few large gulps, before setting the empty bottle on the nightstand.

"Just be careful," Philipe tells me. "Once

you do something, you can never go back." I know he's only looking out for me, but I've lived with the anger for five years, and now that she's here, I'll make sure I get my penance. Since I can't see the regret in her father's eyes, it will have to be my little flower that pays.

She'll pay her debt to the Lancasters for what the Miltons did.

TWELVE

Dahlia

THE WARMTH OF THE HOUSE IS CALMING, IT FEELS like home. My run-in with Ares has my blood hot from frustration and desire. Why he's taunting me, I don't know. I wanted to talk to him about my father, about our families, but with his friend there, it felt awkward.

I have a feeling Etienne does know about the feud between our families, but I wanted privacy. To be alone with Ares. Perhaps I could get through to him. Maybe I can learn who I really am. Because right now, it feels as if I'm a stranger looking in on my life, and I don't recognize myself.

Gran strolls into my bedroom with a mug of hot coffee and a side plate filled with chocolate chip cookies. One of my favorite confections.

"How was school?"

"Fine." My response is more clipped than I wanted, and her graying brow arches in question. I didn't want to tell her, but now I feel I have to.

She stares at me, long and hard, and I wonder if she's going to forbid me to go out. Perhaps Dad told her about me being a homebody, not going out at all. But now that I'm here, I'd like to learn about who I am, about my past.

"Just remember what I told you. Be careful who you trust in this town," Gran finally tells me as she settles herself on my bed. There's a far-off look in her eyes, and I wonder if she's thinking about what Dad had been through while he lived here.

"Does this have something to do with Dad?"

At my question, her gaze snaps to mine, guilt flashes in her eyes before it's gone, her face turning to stone right before me. "Your father was a good man."

"He was, but that doesn't mean he didn't make mistakes," I counter. Deep down, I know my father wasn't a saint. Even though he caught the bad guys, there must've been things he'd done in his youth that he may regret now. If he were still alive.

"Dahlia," she says my name with so much affection, it stills my heart for a moment. I'd only ever met her twice as I was growing up, but the way she's looking at me right now, it makes me feel as if I'm not alone. "There are many secrets in this town, far too many to even fathom. And your father had his fair share of mistakes he made while he lived here."

"Is that why he moved?"

She's silent, contemplative, as she looks at the soft burgundy carpet. I wonder if she's going to respond. "He moved because he had to."

"What does that mean?"

"Just be careful," she says, rising from the bed and offering me a smile before turning to the doorway.

"Yes, Gran," I sigh, knowing I won't get

the answers I seek from her. No. I'm going to have to ask Ares or even his dad. One of them has to tell me what the hell is going on. I watch her walk down the hallway, and I wonder how my life here is going to play out with her watching over me. Not only that, I have Rukaiya's dad who's probably going to be keeping tabs on us all the time as well.

Gran returns, holding a photo album, and sets it on the bed beside me. When she turns to regard me, her expression reminds me so much of Dad that it makes my chest ache.

"I'm just looking out for you, Lia," she admits. I know she loves me, but I'm here, and I don't need to be coddled. I've spent my life growing up with a man who went out and spent time in dangerous situations.

"Nothing is going to happen to me in this tiny town, Gran," I say, immediately regretting it because I don't want her to think I don't appreciate what she's done for me. "I just... I feel as if he's here all the time. It's as if he's not gone at all."

Her gaze lands on mine, and she nods

slowly and smiles. "I know, child," she admits. "At times, I wonder if I remember him. That's why I keep all these small mementos because… He was my son, but he was so independent. Don't think badly of him for what he did, how he raised you. He just wanted you safe."

"I know he did, even though he didn't like me worrying about him," I tell her. "Each time he walked out the door, he made sure I would be okay if something happened to him."

There were times I wondered if my father would come home. He worked in organizations alongside men who were violent, lethal, and dangerous. His job took him places I didn't know about, he met people who could easily kill him, and one day, they did.

"He loved you." Gran's voice is low, whispered, and I wonder if she knew he wasn't coming home. I wonder if she ever worried about him the way I did. Perhaps in a slightly different aspect, but did she know he wouldn't be here for my graduation.

He'd never been one for affection. Perhaps he was getting me ready for the pain, for the loneliness of not having him around. Maybe he knew that his time was up, and soon, I'd have to go on without him.

"I love him, too, he's my dad, I will always love him." I glance at my grandmother.

She smiles sadly and nods. "I'll leave you to it." Slowly, she rises and makes her way out of my room, pulling the door shut behind her. Once I'm alone. I lie back and stare at the ceiling, my mind replaying Ares' invite from yesterday. All day today, I'd been free of his lingering gaze. Each class that passed, it became apparent that he wasn't going to be at school.

Even in History, he wasn't alongside his dad, who taught us about the history of the town and then sprung a random project on us. A fifteen-thousand-word paper, which needs to be handed in on Monday.

When we finished for the day, I was admittedly disappointed that I didn't see Ares. Even though he annoys me, I sort of missed having him follow me around. Whenever he looks as me, there's a glimmer of emotion that makes my body turn hot.

It's strange. Having his attention on me for no reason has piqued my curiosity. Rolling over, I pull out my diary and grab a pen from the nightstand. Opening it to the last page, I allow my words to flow, scrawling in my left-handed script a random idea for my paper.

I love putting it down in ink, then heading to my computer to actually get all the words down. It's how I've always done my school papers, and I love how my mind plays out the scenes like a film reel.

My phone beeps, vibrating on the mattress with an alert. I grab it, unlocking it with my thumbprint, and open the app. Frowning, I notice it's a private number, but I open the message.

Tonight. Seven pm. If you want answers, come alone. Directions attached.

Tapping the link, I take note of the small blue line on the map that shows that the location is not far from where I am right now.

Informing me of the time it will take — a fifteen-minute walk.

There's no name, no indication of who it's from, but I have an idea. For some inexplicable reason, I have a feeling it's Ares. I'm not sure why he'd want me to meet him out in the middle of nowhere, and I really shouldn't go, but my curiosity wins out.

You'll get answers when you come to me, little flower. I want to see you.

It is him.

And even though I know my father would have a heart attack if he knew I was doing this, I ignore the niggling in my gut. All I have to do is tell Gran I'm heading to Rukaiya's. I need answers.

My decision is made.

THIRTEEN

Dahlia

PULLING ON MY HOODIE, I COVER MY HEAD and make my way down the stairs to the road, which leads out of the main town and away from the school buildings, which sit like looming gods, watching over the town.

I wanted to take my car, but a walk may be better for me. I haven't had a chance to think about anything my gran told me, and I haven't opened the photo album she set in my bedroom. Honestly, I'm afraid to see my father's face. He's gone. I'm alone, and I don't know how to think about him without the pain slicing through my chest.

I offer a smile to a few people I pass on my way up toward the hill. The forest here is thick with looming trees, which are losing their leaves. Even as we near October, there's still green scattered about. But I know soon, there'll be a heavy layer of snow over the whole town.

A quick glance over my shoulder is confirmation that I'm now leaving the perimeter of the town and heading just outside the edge. Gran's house seems so far away. I told her I was taking a walk to see Rukaiya. Lying to her isn't something I wanted to do, but I didn't have a choice. If I told her I was meeting Ares, she would ask me hundreds of questions that I don't have the answers for.

I'm not sure why I'm going. At least, that's what I tell myself, but I know it's because the questions that are burning my tongue need answers, and I have a feeling only he can give them to me. Also, I put it down to my curious nature. The same one that my father told me I get from my mother.

Music blares in my ears as I head toward the small dirt road, which snakes through the trees, and as Fall Out Boy sings to me about the fourth of July, a clearing greets me beyond the darkness of the trees. Even though it's fall, it's not completely dark yet, but there's an eeriness to the church that sits in front of me.

I'm half expecting mist to start collecting as I near the building. It's old, three spires shoot to the sky, the bricks are dark and dirty, and the metal that surrounds the stained-glass windows flakes with the old paint that's peeling from it.

The place is practically falling apart, crumbling in areas that should be strong and formidable. A few of the windows are broken, and I wonder what it looks like inside.

Pulling out my earphones, I listen for a rustling or any noise for that matter, but I'm met with silence. Nothing more than the soft breaths from my lips. As I near the church, my phone alerts me to a message.

Good girl. Come inside, we're waiting.

Confusion settles in my gut like a lead weight. I should leave. I really should turn around and run away, but then I notice the black Audi R8 Spyder parked on the left side of the building.

Ares.

I make my way up the steps while rolling my eyes at his games and step inside the empty, eerie building. The doors creak behind me when I step into the musty space, but still, I find nobody when I enter. Instead, I'm met with dust and cobwebs. The dimming light streams through the stained-glass windows, and where some of them are shattered, they offer more of the reddish-golden hue of the sunset than the others.

"Is this your way of scaring me?" I call out, my voice echoing, bouncing off the walls. "Are we playing hide and seek?" I say to the emptiness. When I reach the altar, I notice one deep red flower, a dahlia, sitting on the top step.

The moment I pick it up, a needle pierces my fingertip, causing me to gasp as the prick sends a tingle of pain through my finger. A droplet of blood appears, and I press my thumb to my mouth to lick it clean.

There's a small note attached to the flower with an emblem of a crown on it. But nothing more, not even a hint of where he is or why he's doing this. My chest aches from my heart thudding wildly against my ribs. A soft whoosh sounds behind me, causing me to spin on my heel and there, hidden in the shadows, is a figure.

"Ares?" I step back, almost tripping on a broken tile on the steps of the altar.

The figure doesn't respond, and when he steps out from the darkness, I notice the black cloak with the golden crown, which sits atop his head, even though it's covered with a hood of the same material.

"Welcome," the deep voice sounds, but it's not Ares. I glance to my left as another figure appears. There are two of them now, one on my right, the other nearing from the opposite corner.

Stepping backward, I attempt to put distance between us, but I don't run. I'm worried if I do, they'll both be much quicker than I am, and I don't stand a chance fighting f two of them.

"Ares, this isn't funny," I tell him, but I'm not sure which one is him. They're both wearing gilded crowns, both dressed in these black robes, their faces obscured by thick heavy hoods.

"Little Flower," the one on my left says. "You shouldn't have come here," he tells me.

"You told me to come." My brows furrow, and I'm met with a chuckle.

"This town is ours, and you're not welcome," he says, his voice rigid, and I can't tell if it's Ares toying with me or if it's his friend I saw with him yesterday. The one who flirted with Rukaiya.

"I don't understand," I mutter, confusion heavy in my tone. "What do you mean I'm not welcome? It's a free country—"

"This town belongs to us, you're an outsider who will pay for the sins of the elder who came before you," *he* warns me.

"What do you mean? Did my father do something? Please tell me what happened." I'm nearing the door as I back away slowly, but deep down, I feel as if it's a trick. They know I'm going to try to run, and perhaps they're even planning on it. I can feel the cool breeze against my back, and I know if I can just get outside, I can make a run for it. If I can get myself amongst the trees, I'll be good. I'm cursing myself for not taking my car.

I'm about to pivot when I feel hands grip me from behind, eliciting a scream from my lips, which bounces against the walls, against the glass, and hits back at us. I'm lifted—as if I were merely a rag doll—and held in the air.

In an attempt to kick, I make contact with the person behind me, and a grunt of pain makes me smile. He releases me, and I make my escape, but I'm not fast enough, not by a long shot, and a hand grips my ankle, pulling me to the floor with a thud that causes my teeth to grit against each other.

The way my body falls on the concrete floor sends pain lancing through my entire body, especially my hip. I'm curled in agony then dragged across the dirty surface until I'm back at the altar. Dust clouds around me, nd I can't stop the sneezing and coughing fit, which attacks me.

"Even though you aren't welcome in our town, you should stay," another voice, a deeper, more gravelly one states. "Because then, you can play our little game until you've paid for the sins of your father," he tells me.

"I... I don't know what you're talking about," I bite out in frustration and fear. The two emotions warring against each other as I claw my way forward, a stupid attempt at escape, which I know is futile.

"We do like the chase," I recognize Ares' voice the moment the words are uttered. "Well, I do in any event."

"Why are you doing this?" I cry out when a foot lands on my leg, keeping me in place, making it impossible to keep fighting. I can't move, so I lie back, waiting for more pain, but it doesn't come. Instead, I feel the heat of his gaze, and when the original figure steps closer to me, I notice those familiar hazel eyes.

"You, little flower, are mine now," he tells me. "You walked into my town, thinking you're safe." The words he speaks, the tone of his voice is cold, indifferent as if he doesn't care about me.

Why would he? He doesn't know me.

"Why are you doing this? I haven't done anything to warrant your—"

"All things will come to light soon enough, little flower," he interrupts me, crouching down, so his face is right in front of mine. The glint of the last bit of light flickers on the crown which sits atop his head.

"Why not tell me now?" Tipping my head to the side, I watch him. The hood shadows most of his face, but it's his smirk that's clear as day.

He reaches for my chin, gripping it painfully between his thumb and forefinger, holding me steady as he closes the distance between us. I half expect him to kiss me, and I don't know why I want that, but instead, he laughs in my face as if I'm stupid.

"You know what," I bite out, wincing when he pinches my chin. "Fuck you. I don't have to do shit for you."

"Don't fuck with me, little flower." His voice is low, a warning clear in his words. He could hurt me. He has two strong friends beside him, and I'm alone. I may be able to fight, but I can't take all three.

He lowers himself over me, pinning me to the cold hard floor under him as his heavy body hovers over mine. Every nerve sparks with electric energy when he presses his knee between my thighs, causing a soft whimper to fall from my lips.

"That's it, flower, I plan to pluck you petal by precious petal." He grins manically. His two hooded friends chuckle loudly at his threat, which angers me, turning my blood hot with rage.

I move quickly, lifting my knee, I make contact with his thigh, missing the place I was aiming for causing him to guffaw, but he doesn't relent. He doesn't move; instead, he stays over me, warming and cooling me at the same time.

"Mmm, she likes it rough," he murmurs in my face. His lips trail over mine, causing electricity to shoot through every nerve ending in my body. But he doesn't press a kiss to my mouth, instead he finds my cheek, then peppers a hot path to my ear. "I like it rough, too, little flower."

It's a promise.

A vow.

And I don't know why my body responds, but it does.

"Leave me alone, please," I plead once more.

Swiftly, he moves, and when I open my eyes, he's standing over me, dropping a red dahlia on my stomach as he and both his friends saunter off, leaving me in the abandoned building with my heart stuck in my throat.

FOURTEEN

Ares

I REACH THE HALLWAY, TAKING THE STEPS TWO AT a time; I know I'm in shit for being late for the meeting, but fuck it, my dick was hard toying with Dahlia.

The fear in her eyes was like an aphrodisiac.

And I plan to see it there a lot more before she learns the truth.

Pulling out my phone, I open the tracker and note that little Dahlia is at home. When we had her in the church, I made sure to get the device attached to her phone. A small, lightweight sticker that holds millions of tiny cables allows me to track her.

Tarian is a genius when technology, and he comes in handy when I need shit found out. He can hack into any computer system, and that's why he's my father's head of IT at only twenty years old.

I know he'll help me keep eyes on her. With his expertise, she won't be able to go to the restroom without me knowing. I smile as I think back to the moment that I had her pinned beneath me. My mind still running images of her lips on mine on a never-ending loop. Her mouth felt like fire and ice, the need to claim her and kill her ran rampant through me.

Stepping through the doors, I inhale the waxy scent of the candles and note my brother sitting at the head of the table. His gaze is on the screen of his iPad, but he glances up when I near him.

"It's about time."

"You didn't tell me I had a curfew." I shrug as I slide into the chair to the right of Philipe.

Philipe shakes his head, ignoring me for a moment, before lifting his gaze and meeting mine. "Don't be a smartass," he bites out, sliding the device over the table toward me without saying another word.

I pick it up, scanning the information

about Patrick Milton's death, which has now hit the papers. I scroll through the pages and nod.

"Do you want me to call Etienne and Tarian?" I question, pulling out my phone.

"No, Dad has already called them. They should be on their way," he murmurs, lowering his voice as if people can hear us in the dungeon. But where we're seated, nobody can find us. This sacred place, hidden from others, will never be found. And that's how the ancestors wanted it.

It's where I will be for the rest of my life if the gold nameplate that's screwed to the heavy wooden table is anything to go by. The old tradition hasn't died out. With every new recruit, an emblazoned nameplate is made of metal to show that once you're in the Sovereign, you never leave.

Even once you retire like our old man, you're still a Sovereign.

The moment I think of him, he enters wearing his cloak and hood. I can't help smiling when he sets down the ink and gun.

It's time. The door creaks and two more figures saunter in—Etienne and Tarian.

"Welcome Sovereign," Father says with a smirk. He settles himself in the seat at the head of the table opposite Philipe. "The Elder Crowns wanted to be here, but there has been an incident that they needed to deal with."

Etienne's gaze snaps toward my father before he questions, "What happened?"

"It seems Kelli has taken ill." The response isn't what I was expecting. "Harding will be spending time with his daughter for a few weeks."

"She was at school today," I inform dad, confused at what could've happened that she suddenly ended up sick within a matter of hours.

"I spoke to Leonard earlier, he's taking Kelli to the city that's why I was taking his class today," Father informs us. "Now, let's get this going." He picks up the gun, setting out the ink. "Are you ready?" His gaze is locked on mine, and I nod.

"I was born ready." I chuckle, unbuttoning

the shirt I'm wearing. I thought I'd have to be dressed up for this evening, but it seems I'm overdressed.

Dad rises, making his way toward me. I push my chair backward and turn around, so my back is to him. Leaning my arms on the back of the seat, I rest my forehead on them and wait.

Growing up with the man who is the head of The Gilded Sovereign has been a challenge. I've had to keep the secret since I turned sixteen, and soon, I'll be twenty-one when I'm officially welcomed into the society. An age-old group of men who run everything and everyone.

My father is one of the most important men in the country. When he's not sitting comfortably in his office at home, he's traveling the country meeting with investors who want to make billions with new software.

Lancaster Corporation is an IT and Communications company that runs all encrypted data for agencies that need privacy. He is the Elder who has been at the head of the table since he turned twenty-one.

Since then, he's been working with the three other members who've since stepped down, ensuring the contacts we have across the world get anything they need on time. These men hold the secret of the Sovereign, but if we call on them, they can bury any activity that takes place—illegal or not—and that's why they're the same men who run countries around the world.

Hackers can't break into my father's software. But I can. And I'm going to find out all I can about my little flower. There will be nothing she can hide from me.

The buzzing of the gun starts, and soon, the bite of pain from the needle eats into my skin. I close my eyes, picturing Dahlia. Her long dark hair, her pretty blue eyes that were filled with worry. I ache for more, to make her feel that emotion of fear every single day of her life.

As my father tattoos me, I think back to *that* night.

A knock at the door wakes me from a dreamless sleep. When my eyes snap open, I'm in bed, the patterns in the ceiling still swirling above me, meaning the alcohol is still racing through my bloodstream.

I recall the night before, or is it still night? I don't know.

Last night's party is still fresh in my mind. I can't believe Etienne was able to get those girls to join us. His parents had been visiting with mine. They didn't tell me what it was about, and when I questioned Dad, he told me to mind my own business.

I know he's hiding secrets from me. Something Philipe said before he left has made me cautious of my father's meetings.

Sixteen. I'm fucking sixteen, and I still have to be treated like a fucking child. I have to prove myself for no fucking reason. I have a feeling it's about the society, the secrets my father hides. The whispers that are filtering around the school has to be about the Sovereign.

"You walked out, I will never be able to have you return to the Sovereign." My father's voice

is cold and rigid, which has me jolting upright. I knew something woke me, but I wasn't sure what. Now I know.

"I need protection," a female voice, not my mother's, responds.

Shooting up from my bed, I make my way to the door. They must be in the hallway, or I wouldn't be able to hear them otherwise. My door is still shut, and I know the moment I try to open it, they'll realize that I'm awake.

Pressing my ear to the wooden surface, I close my eyes and focus. Everything is silent for a long while before I hear shuffling and footsteps.

"I brought this for you," the female speaks again.

More silence.

"Where did you find this?"

"He kept it in a safe," she tells my father. I don't recognize the voice, so it can't be anyone I've met before. I wish I could see through the fucking walls right now.

"You stole it?" Dad bites out, the anger in his tone is palpable. When my father gets angry, nothing can calm him down. He's like one of those goddamned guard dogs that gets lockjaw on his prey.

"I had to. I need your help, please? She should be here. Protected by you."

I'm not sure what my father is doing, but then I hear more shuffling, and the soft footfalls disappear. Taking a chance, I twist the doorknob and tug it open slowly. The hallway is empty, and I realize they've probably gone down to his office.

My bare feet move toward the staircase when I hear the front door click. There's no sound until I hear the gun cocking and a shot ring through the almost empty house. I race down the steps and see a man smirking at my father who's now clutching his shoulder.

"Dad!"

"Ares, get the fuck upstairs, now!" My father's tone booms through the large open space and I don't want to obey him, but my feet are already moving. "I said now!" Once more, his rage is like a vise on me, dragging me back to my bedroom.

That man isn't here for me, or he would've shot me. He's here for my father. Shutting my eyes, I focus on the carpet, trying not to puke. My stomach roils when I think of that asshole killing my father.

Grabbing my phone, I hit dial on Etienne's number. The second he answers, I'm rambling an explanation about what's happening downstairs. Even though he lives on the opposite side of town, it won't take Etienne and Tarian long to get here.

"Tell your dad to get here now," I inform my best friend. I know that Mr. Durand is part of the society, and he'll do anything to keep my dad safe. Anything.

There are more shouts and arguing, and I can just about make out the words. The man sounds livid, and dad sounds like he's about to kill the asshole with threats so volatile I'm shivering.

A door opens and closes, soft hushed footfalls sound again. My brows are furrowed when I pull open my bedroom door and exit into the hallway. I breathe deeply when I hear the woman speaking again.

"She's meant to be here!"

"Like fuck she is," my father grits out. I don't know who they're talking about, but I will find out. I'm sure Dad has secrets hiding in his office.

It only takes ten minutes for the front door to

fly open, and Etienne's dad to saunter in. "What the fuck are you doing back here?" Mr. Durand's tone is thunder. Etienne isn't with him, and I wonder where my best friend is.

"I came back to finish off what you started," the man utters, pure hate filling his words, and I'm even more confused. I've never seen him before.

"You should never have come back here. I told you—"

"You no longer rule my life," the stranger bites out, interrupting my father. His rage is like an entity of its own. I want to go out there to face this asshole, but I know Dad will lose his shit, and I'll be grounded.

Frustration gnaws at me, anxiety twisting painfully in my stomach. My gut heavy, filled with the pain of not knowing how to help them. I can't let them know I'm here.

"Alexander." This comes from my mother, who I realize was the person I heard leaving the bedroom moments ago. "Why are you here? You walked out, left us," she tells him in a calm tone, ever the peacemaker.

"You forced my hand," the man, Alexander,

168

says.

"We did no such thing; the Sovereign is sacred."

"Sacred my fucking ass, this ends tonight."
Alexander's words are filled with rage.

I sneak a peek around the edge of the wall that's hiding me. When my gaze lands on the scene, I have to fight the urge to shout. The man is now pointing the gun at my mother who doesn't look scared at all.

"You're really going to do this?" She asks him as if they're old friends. As if she knew he was coming here and that he's only waving a fucking gun around for the fun of it.

"This wasn't the life I wanted. It's wrong, this fucked up society you think governs the country, the world, you're all using it for your own benefit, not for the average man out on the street," the man utters with loathsome undertones.

"That's it, son," Dad speaks, and I'm torn back to the present. "Etienne, are you ready?"

"Yes, sir," my best friend grins playfully, and I know he's as excited as I am for this.

"Once your birthdays roll around, you will each receive a copy of the *book*. It's not long now that each of you turns twenty-one, and you'll have access to contacts anywhere in the world," Philipe tells us with a satisfied smirk.

"I think we should have a party this weekend since I've already invited a few people," I inform him. My brother is older, more responsible, and even though he's a lot more level headed than I am, there are times he lets loose.

The moment he left, he built a life outside the stuffy suits we've grown up with. Every time we've had an event at home or at the school, it's been formal, black tie, which is bullshit.

My brother nods. "Perhaps. I'll think about it." The green of my brother's eyes shimmer with curiosity at my sudden need for a party, but I know what's bothering him right now—wondering if he can ever fill our father's shoes.

"Don't fuck up the house," Dad warns us

as he inks Etienne on the bicep. The ink is dark, mingled with the crimson of blood. I watch mesmerized by the movement and sound of the gun whirring.

"Are we adding any more Sovereigns after Etienne and Tarian?" I question. Even though we're the main part of the Sovereign, there are more across the world. Each of the men who join are well-known—senators, presidents, actors, and musicians.

They use the contacts we've collected over the years to move up the ladder, so to speak. We own everything: government, law enforcement, even the Cartel answers to us. If we don't sign off on it, a deal doesn't happen.

Philipe shrugs, glancing between Dad and me before responding, "I don't believe so. For now, the four of us will become the new leaders, and the rest of them are required to obey the orders that come down from the head of the table."

In each country, the Sovereign have their own societies; some cities have up to twelve: all between the ages of twenty-one and thirty.

The older ones are Elders, leading the younger. But here in America, we rule them all. We set out the law, and they follow.

I'm lost in thought as I hear the buzzing of the needle, which soothes the tension in my shoulders. Responsibility comes with having the tattoo, being one of the Crowns. Even though I enjoy parties, and I do stupid shit at times like fighting at Billy's, there's always something that brings me back to the dungeon, to the church.

Knowing I'm part of something my ancestors started so many years ago is jarring because I have to uphold the Lancaster name. Even though Philipe is also at the table, I feel as if I have a lot to prove being the younger sibling.

I glance at Etienne, watching as the needle dances along his skin. Thankfully, I have two of my best friends along for the ride. I don't know if I ever could have done this alone.

They were there for me when I didn't think I needed anyone. We're not only friends, we're brothers. Blood doesn't always necessarily mean family.

Those you choose can be more important to you than those who are related by blood and genes. The ones who stand by you even when you do stupid shit and don't judge you.

I don't know how long I'm lost in thought, but Etienne stands and turns to show off his ink. His shoulder blade holds the promise that no matter what, we will always be there for each other.

I couldn't have chosen a better family.

Dad cuts his gaze toward me as Tarian moves to get his ink done. "You need to listen to your brother," he tells me, something he's voiced all my life. I'm so used to it.

I can't help but smirk at his wariness. "You don't trust me, Dad?" I push up, rising to full height.

"It's not that," Philipe responds. "This is something I take seriously, Ares. You're volatile; I'm just ensuring you don't lose your shit. You're strong," he informs me of what I already know. "War isn't something we need to be starting with law enforcement. We've always worked with them, keeping our heads down, and our names out of trouble. Let's not give them too much work before you've held your Crown."

"I know, brother," I tell him, leaning over the table with my palms flat on the cool wooden surface, and lock my gaze with his. "Listen, I'm grown up. I may not be as grown-up or as vigilant as you, but I know what I'm doing." Our gazes lock, once more, and there's no doubt I should be shoved off this table, but I know Philipe wouldn't do that to me. "Anyway, I better head out, I have something to do."

He nods. "Fine. Just don't get into trouble tonight."

I can't help but laugh as I make my way to the door. I look forward to what I'm heading out to do, but trouble… that finds me, not the other way around.

I glance at my best friends and offer them a two-finger salute. I told them my plan, and they both agreed. Etienne offers me a wink before I turn and walk outside.

The evening air is balmy as I make my way to my *sweet ride*—the Maserati that my dad gifted me when I turned eighteen. Even though my Audi looks lonely, tonight, we're going VIP, and that calls for a slick ride.

The engine purrs when I hit the gas and speed down the drive toward the gates. They slide open, allowing me to exit, and soon, I'm headed down toward the second largest property in the town we call our home. Etienne's family's plot sits on the opposite side of town as if we're guarding the place.

I smile when I notice the girls walking around the campus in short skirts and tank tops. I love summer, and I'm feeling rather adventurous tonight.

"This is the life," I utter to myself with a smile when two pretty blondes smile over at me the moment they meet my hungry gaze. All heads turn when I speed down the road with my music blaring and the wind whipping through my unruly hair.

I pull up to the road that sits behind Dahlia's grandmother's house and kill the engine. Glancing at the window that I know is her bedroom, I notice the light flickering, and I wonder if she's lying on her bed, and with that comes an image of her in nothing but a pair of panties and a tank top, which makes me groan.

"Hello, Little Flower, time for us to talk."

FIFTEEN

Dahlia

THE DIM YELLOW LAMP ILLUMINATES MY ROOM. The brass double bed sits against the dark green wall, which has a small cream-colored arch built into it that juts out slightly. Beside me to the right, alongside the window, is a floor to ceiling bookshelf, which overlooks the university in the distance, and the forest beyond.

The dark wooden floor is covered in rich brown and red mats: there's one by the bed and one beside my window seat. A small desk sits opposite my bed and beside the door, which leads out onto the hallway.

A clink on the window takes my attention away from the latest romance novel I'd gotten lost in. I still all movement, training my ears to listen for another clink, or something similar. When I don't hear a sound, I cast my gaze back to the book.

"Little Flower." Ares's voice jolts me from the bed, causing my heart to leap into my throat. I'm on my feet in the next second, painfully aware of the way I'm dressed. He's sitting on the window ledge with his dark booted feet on top of the soft cushion of my window seat.

"What the hell are you—"

"If you alert her that I'm here in your bedroom, she'll be angrier at you than me," he tells me with confidence, gesturing with his chin toward the door. I know he's right. Gran's already warned me against this asshole. If she walks in here now, I'll be grounded, even though I'm almost nineteen. She would probably lock me in the house to keep me out of trouble.

"What do you want? Didn't you toy with me enough earlier?" I bite out, crossing my arms in front of my chest to cover up the fact that I'm not wearing a bra. But it's useless because those honey-colored eyes lock on my hardened nipples. His lips curl into a dark, sinister smirk.

"Well, I'll happily oblige you and your pretty breasts," Ares says, rising like a predator, slow and meticulous. He quickly closes the distance between us with a few long strides, and the moment my back hits the wall beside my desk, I'm caged in.

"Don't be an asshole," I bite out, placing my palms against his chest—which I realize the moment I make contact with his body— was a mistake. Electricity shoots through me, turning my body molten. *Why the hell do I have such an innate response to him?*

"I thought you were already convinced I was," he says, tipping his head to the side as he regards me. A flash of amusement passes across his handsome features, and I have to focus on what happened earlier to stop myself from leaning into him.

His sharp, angular jaw with a light dusting of stubble makes my fingers tingle to touch him. His chiseled cheekbones give way to full lips and a sharp nose. His eyes are almost luminous in the dim light of my room with the green flecks turning dark and foreboding.

He's so close I have to tip my head back to look at him. Lean muscles, broad shoulders, and tapered hips are the only evidence that he's clearly defined with dips and peaks of toned muscle under the tight shirt he's wearing.

Shaking out of my stupor, I retort, "I am. I was giving you a chance to be nice to me. To explain why you hate me." My voice cracks on the last few words, which causes me to cringe, because I don't want him to know his dislike for me means more than it should.

"I don't need to explain myself to anyone, especially the likes of you." The sneer that turns his face into a cruel mask makes my chest ache as his words hit me deep. He leans into me, his body looming over mine. Both his palms are flat against the wall on either side of my head, and his mouth is inches from mine. I can't stop my gaze from tracking the curl of his lips or from realizing how full the bottom one is compared to the top.

Lifting my stare to meet his, I note how the green flecks that are almost invisible with how dark they are, turning the hazel a deep caramel as he watches me through his thick lashes.

"Then it's best you leave," I manage to croak out. My throat feels thick, while my heart beats a harsh rhythm against my ribs. His cologne envelops me, and I'm almost intoxicated by the fragrance. My hands are still on his chest, the heat searing me as if he's trying to either burn me off him or melt me into him.

"What if I don't want to leave?" His question stills me for a second, causing me to frown. The glint in his gaze lights a fire in my gut, the flames lick my insides, turning them molten with equal amounts of fear and desire. "I enjoy seeing your eyes fill with fear and trepidation."

"I'm not scared of you," I bite out, pushing against him harder this time, and he allows me room to breathe. "I've grown up with danger surrounding me -- you're nothing compared to what I have been through."

"Oh?" Ares seems intrigued by this. "And what sort of danger have you been in, little flower?" he questions, arching a dark brow at me. He folds his arms in front of his chest, and his gaze narrows, focusing on me like a predator to his prey. And every part of my body, from the tips of my toes to the roots of my long dark hair, feels his stare.

"I've lived with the threat of losing not only my mother but my father and myself to criminals. My father has put away a lot of bad men, and I was always a target when they learned who my dad was," I retort, unsure of why I'm explaining myself to him. He doesn't deserve it, but I don't like the fact that he thinks he can scare me.

"Your father..." The seething tone of his voice sends a cold shiver racing down my spine. Silence hangs heavily around us, thick with rage and fury.

"Your hate runs so deep. Nothing can etch it out." It's not a question. But something about the way Ares glances at me tells me I'm right. "Why is it you hate me so much when I haven't done anything to you?"

"This isn't... I should go." He spins on his heel, turning toward the window, but this time, it's me who reaches out to him. I grab his arm, the warmth of him turning me hot. "Let go of me, flower," he bites out, anger fueling his words.

"Tell me, Ares," I hiss in frustration. *Why won't anyone tell me who my father really was when he lived here?* "Don't I deserve to know why you hate the man who raised me?"

"You're his blood, you don't deserve shit from me," Ares spins around, gripping my shoulders, holding me hostage with the glare he's pinned me with. He takes a deep, long inhale before he grins. "Well, maybe I can make an exception and fuck you before I end you."

"W-wh-what?" The word falls aimlessly from my lips, shock lacing every syllable.

Ares' gaze burns me as he takes in my now visible cleavage, trailing a white-hot path with his eyes from my chest up to my face.

"You should pay for what your family did to mine. Since you're the last remaining Milton alive," he sneers, as his fingers dig deeper into the soft flesh of my arms. I'll be bruised tomorrow, of that I'm sure.

"You're sick," I spit the words in his face, causing his smirk to lift and curl as if a sleeping serpent is about to awaken. Ares shoves me against the wall once more, pressing his whole body against mine. Head to toe, I'm covered by him. Every hard ridge of him is against me, and that's when he nudges his hips to taunt me.

A whimper falls from my lips when I feel his erection. I'm wet. My panties are soaked, and there's nothing I can do to stop the electricity shooting through every nerve in my body.

"It seems my little flower is sick, too," he whispers along my neck and jaw until he reaches my ear. "Don't worry, Dahlia, I'll give you what you need." As he speaks, he rolls his hips, again and again, causing my body to tremble with anticipation. Even though I don't want this—at least I tell myself that—it seems my body has a mind of its own because it reacts to Ares, needing the release he's taunting me with.

The tightness in my belly knots and tugs at my restraint and my fingers curl into fists. My nails dig half-moons into my palm to keep myself from begging him for more.

"Is that what you want?" Ares mocks me as his gravelly tone feathers in my ear. His hot breath fanning the flames that are slowly building within me. Bright white sparks dance against my lids as I attempt to curb the desire I feel in this completely fucked up situation.

"Get the fuck out," I murmur, but there's no conviction in my voice. I can't do this. He's toying with me, turning me into a melting pot of desire and rage. "I hate you."

"Good. It will make this war so much more fun. An enjoyable battle can only be played between people who hate each other." He growls. *He fucking growls.*

Suddenly, I'm ice cold because he steps away. My eyes snap open, taking in the man who's turned me inside out in a mere few minutes of contact. He turns, and I can't stop staring at the smirk that curls his perfect lips. My gaze is locked on him, watching as his body moves toward my window. Without a backward glance, he's gone, and I'm left alone in my room wondering what the hell just happened.

On trembling legs, I race to the window, but the darkness has swallowed him up, and all I see are the tiny pinpricks of lights at the school and the stars in the sky. Even the moon has disappeared behind clouds.

"Shit," I bite out in frustration.

I have to find out why he hates my dad so much. Nothing makes sense. I know there has to be a truth that nobody is brave enough to offer me. I'm not a fragile flower like Ares seems to think I am.

If I can push Ares far enough, perhaps he'll finally gift me the truth I deserve. It's as if everyone is trying to keep me safe by not telling me what I so clearly should know, and I'm tired of it. I'm done with being treated like

I'm breakable because I'm far from it.

Did dad really do something so bad to deserve Ares' family's hatred?

Was he hiding something from me all this time?

I need to find out. And Ares is going to tell me.

SIXTEEN

Ares

I SHOULDN'T HAVE DONE THAT. FUCK.

"Where have you been?" Philipe questions as soon as I walk into the kitchen. I came straight home after seeing her because my dick is hard, my balls are blue, and all I wanted was to claim her against the wall of her pretty bedroom.

"Out."

"You seem… tense," my brother remarks in a tone that sets me on edge.

Of course, I'm fucking tense.

"Why do you care?" I bite out, opening the bottle of beer I pulled out of the fridge. Snapping off the metal cap, I turn to regard Philipe.

He shrugs, but there's amusement dancing

in his eyes. It's clear that older brothers are put on earth to fuck with their younger siblings. I've lived with it all my life, but this time, I'm done with his bullshit.

"Tell me," I utter as I settle opposite him. He's working on his laptop, but he closes it the moment I'm seated. "I should be looped in on everything. Shouldn't I?" The skin where the ink has been emblazoned on me tinges when I think about it.

"The girl," Philipe says on a sigh, lifting the beer to his lips before taking a long gulp. I watch him swallow down the liquid. "She's getting to you."

"She's not—"

"Brother, I've seen a man whipped, I've been there and done that," he tells me, leaning back against his chair. His eyes, usually a shade of bright green, are dark, filled with confidence as he tells me this.

"You? Interested in only one girl," I chuckle. "That doesn't sound like the brother I know."

It's true. Philipe's well-known in this

town for fucking every girl in his year of high school, heading to college to get his degree and getting into the panties of every freshman and senior until he moved to New York.

"A long time ago, I was someone who wanted a relationship," he admits, and the tinge of pain is laced in his words. "Utter stupidity," Philipe mutters. "Love and all the bullshit that comes with it is pointless. In this life,"—he waves his hand around us— "it's not worth it. Hiding shit from someone who trusts you is not the way to a long-term relationship."

"Since when did you become so focused on love and emotion?" Folding my arms in front of my chest, I watch my brother with curiosity. I don't know why Dahlia has such an effect on me, but she's not someone I'm going to fall in love with.

Not because she's not beautiful, she is. But her father killed my mother in cold blood. That's not something I'll ever forgive.

"I'm not focused on it. I just learned the hard way that being in the Sovereign means you'll be alone forever."

"I'm fine with that," I retort, rising from the chair and heading to the hallway, I need to get away from this conversation.

"You may be fine with it now," Philipe says when I reach the threshold of the kitchen to the hallway, "but in a few years, you'll come to realize this life isn't all it's cracked up to be."

For a moment, I wonder if he's warning me to walk away. But then I remember — I'm marked. The ink on my skin is there forever. I nod, turning and heading to the staircase, which leads up to the second floor.

Once I'm in my bedroom, I shut the door and pull out my phone. Opening the messenger app, I tap out one to Etienne and Tarian to let them know there's a bonfire tomorrow night, and then I send one to my little flower.

Tomorrow at the bonfire, our first battle... Let's see if your petals will burn in the heat.

It doesn't take long for her to respond with

anger and rage, just like I knew she would.

I don't take orders, Lancaster. It doesn't matter who you are or what lies in our past, I will not bow to you and your sick needs.

I crack a smile at her feistiness. I'd never had a woman who was so adamant at hating me, but then again, I'd never been in such turmoil over anyone before. Most of the girls at school throw themselves in my path because they want to be seen. They crave the popularity that the Lancaster name can give them, but I find myself not wanting their attention. Instead, I'm more interested in the blossoming Dahlia than anyone else.

Typing out my response, I hit send before I head into the bathroom and turn on the shower. Stripping down, I glance at the ink and blood that's collected in a pattern around the plastic wrap covering my new tattoo.

Staring at myself in the mirror, I take note of the tattoo that makes me one of the Crowns. The one thing I wanted all my life is now in my hands. But that's not the only thing I crave, there's one more thing that's mine.

The moment I tug the tape holding the plastic wrap, a hiss escapes my clenched teeth. "Fucker," I growl to myself. Opening the cabinet, I find a fresh roll of medical tape and tear off a few pieces. Gently, I work to recover it, making sure it's airtight, so it doesn't get wet.

I step under the spray and let the water massage my tense shoulders before I lather up the rest of my body. My mind is still on a loop, replaying how Dahlia's body trembled beneath mine.

Her soft curves, her sweet perfume, and the way her pupils dilated were evidence enough that she wants me.

How can I crave a woman whose father has done such bad shit to mine?

My eyes close, and I can't stop my hand from dropping to my shaft. Fisting myself, I stroke slowly, edging myself as I picture her delicate hand wrapped around me.

Thinking about her sweetness, her fire,

and her curves, I groan as pleasure zips through me like a lightning strike. My nerves are frayed, my need for her is unacceptable, but I can't stop my hand jerking harder, faster, picturing her plump lips parting for me, and another low growl escapes me when I imagine painting her pretty face with my release.

My body tenses and I call her name as I empty myself down the drain. "This is fucking ridiculous," I murmur at the walls that surround me.

Once I've rinsed off the soap, I shut off the taps and step out onto the soft mat and grab a towel, wrapping it around my waist. Back in the bedroom, I pick up my cell and find a response from Dahlia.

With a grin, I hit dial on her number. Two rings and she answers with a hushed, yet frustrated whisper, "What do you want?"

The screen shows her pretty face, and I can't deny, she's hot; I'd fuck her right now. Shaking my head of the errand thought, I focus on those wide eyes that take me in, realizing I'm half-naked.

"What the fuck are you wearing?" she bites out, louder than her earlier question, which makes me chuckle.

"A towel, you've heard of those where you're from, I assume?" I move across my bedroom, and I know she can see the furnishings—dark and luxurious—behind me.

"What do you want, Ares? I don't have time for games."

"But you play them so well." This makes her still, her face turning angry before my eyes. Her fire does things to me. It makes my towel tent for one thing. "I want you at the bonfire," I tell her. "Let's see who'll play this game and win."

"What do I get if I win?" She succumbs to my command.

"Me."

"What?" Her shock matches my own. *What the fuck am I saying?*

Settling on the soft cushion of the armchair in my room that overlooks the town, I cast my glance out the window before looking at her again. "You'll get to know everything there is about me, my family, and how you tie into it."

"What if I lose?" Her voice cracks on the words, and I want to go to her. Right now, I want to get in my car, drive over there, and skulk into her bedroom. I want to pin her to the bed and show her what she'll get when she loses. My hands wrapped tightly around her neck.

"Are you planning on losing?"

"Just answer the fucking question," she retorts, her mouth pursing in frustration and the shape of those lips makes my cock jolt with need.

"You don't want to know what happens to losers in this town."

"My father did something to you. Didn't he?"

I want to answer her. To give her the truthful response, but I can't. Not yet. There's nothing I can say that will change her fate.

"Ares?"

"Your father isn't the man you think he is." My words are the only response I can offer

196

her at this moment.

"He was a good man."

"Was he?" I challenge her belief, hoping to make her question herself. She watches me over the small screen, and I wonder if she'll ever believe her dear old daddy killed someone. An innocent.

"I-I... he was a cop, he put so many bad people in prison."

"And before he was part of law enforcement? Did you know your dad as well as you think?" This time, she stares at me long and hard, assessing my reaction, my expression, everything about what she can see.

"What did he do?" Her voice is a whisper, husky and sweet, like a tempting treat. I want to swallow it up. I want to devour her inch by inch until there's nothing left but a shell of the woman before me.

I want her to ache for me.

A thought steals my attention for a moment before I swipe it away. I could do something worse than killing her. I could punish her for far longer than a mere few moments of gurgled pleas of mercy.

"You're so fucking full of it, Lancaster," Dahlia bites out, dragging me from my thoughts.

Yes.

A plan formulates in my mind, and I'm soon smiling at her.

"I am. And soon, you'll be full of me, too." I hang up before she has time to respond. "You've just played right into my hand, little flower. Now it's time for war. And you're not going to survive it."

SEVENTEEN
Dahlia

THE RED NUMBERS ON MY ALARM CLOCK TAUNT me.

Four in the morning and I haven't slept a wink. My body is buzzed as if I'd had enough coffee to wake the dead. Something has been bothering me since I spoke to Ares on FaceTime earlier.

Besides the fact that he was half-naked, which was definitely distracting, he said things that didn't make sense. I knew my father was good, he'd always been a great father. Even though he wasn't always present when I needed him, I knew he loved and cared for me. And when my mother left, he was there to pick up the pieces and be both parents.

Granted, there were times I didn't know

where he was. But that was his job. *Wasn't it?* The whole conversation I had with Ares plays over and over in my mind, reminding me that he knows more about my dad than I do. Clearly.

Sighing, I roll over and grab my phone. No new messages. Opening social media, I scroll through my timeline, noting how nothing exciting ever happens in my life. It doesn't help that I only have three hundred friends. All of those are kids from my old school who I never really spoke to in the first place.

Tapping on the search bar, I type in Ares Lancaster and hit the enter key. The moment his profile appears, I find myself enthralled by his photos. Friendly smiles, he and his two friends, Tarian and Etienne, stare into the camera—either alone or with a group of girls.

As I swipe through the albums, I stumble upon a photo of Ares, and another handsome guy appears. I'm sure this is his brother. He looks like a mix of Ares and Abner, their father. He's good-looking, but his eyes, those deep-set green orbs seem haunted.

It's only when I reach the older photos from when they were kids that I find a woman beside Ares in one image that steals my breath. She's beautiful with long blonde hair, wide green eyes, and a smile that lights up the photo.

Me and mom before the picnic.

The tagline grips my chest in a tight-fisted hold, and my breathing becomes erratic. Shoving off the bed, I race to the album my gran left for me. When I flip it open, I find old photos of my dad. Each picture looks old, they even have a soft sepia overlay on them which confirms these were taken years ago, way before I was born. The moment I get to his high school prom, I stumble backward.

Dropping the album, I flop onto the bed and stare at the item on the floor. The photo glaring at me is far too familiar, but at the same time, it's as if it's a mystery. There, smiling back at me is my father, Abner Lancaster, and the beautiful blonde woman from Ares' photo.

I don't know what that means. I'm confused, but yet, deep down in my gut, I'm almost certain that my father had something to do with the fact that this woman is not in any recent shots with her sons.

Setting my phone on the nightstand, I get up and pad over to the door, pulling it open and stepping into the hallway. The house is silent, beside the clock downstairs ticking loudly. The sound echoes up the steps as I make my way to the bathroom, shutting myself inside, and turning on the shower.

Once I've undressed, I step under the hot spray and close my eyes, leaning my head back, reveling in the warmth of the water. My muscles are tense, achy, and I wonder for a moment why.

An image of the church flashes in my mind. The warning Ares gave me compared to his presence last night has confused the hell out of me. Surely, he can just come right out and tell me how he knows my father.

I quickly lather up with my rose fragranced soap and wash my hair. When I step out into the chilly room, a shiver trickles over me, causing goosebumps to rise up over my skin. Wrapping myself in a fluffy towel, I head back to my bedroom and slide open the closet doors.

With a pair of jeans in hand, along with a long-sleeved fitted top, I grab some underwear and socks. As I get dressed, my mind is still on everything that's happened. Once I've slipped on a pair of boots, I pick up my phone to find a message waiting for me.

Flowers blossom at sunrise and wilt in the dark… How are you today, little flower?

Shoving my phone into my pocket, I ignore Ares' attempt at a taunt. I'm done being a toy for Ares and his friends; today, I'll get him to talk. With the photo album in hand, I make my way into the kitchen, set a mug under the Keurig, and breathe deeply to calm my erratic heartbeat.

Once the mug is full, I settle at the kitchen table and stare at the cover of my gran's album that holds secrets I didn't know my father kept. How could he lie to me? Opening to the page I found this morning, I stare at the woman, the blonde, green-eyed woman, who looks so much like her sons. Or they look like her.

Her smile is wide, reminding me of Ares when he didn't know I was watching. The man staring at her, Abner Lancaster, looks like a man besotted. But when I drag my gaze toward my father, what catches my attention is the black snaking out of the shirt cuff onto his wrist.

Furrowing my brow, I lean in further, trying to make out what it is. I remember my father having a scar on his hand, one that looked painful, as if his flesh was sliced open. When I asked him about it, he told me his job was dangerous.

At that time, I believed him. But now, I'm not so sure.

"You're up early," Gran says as she enters the room. She settles opposite me once she's gotten herself a mug of coffee.

"Couldn't sleep," I tell her. I glance up, noting her gaze on the album before me. "Did my dad ever have a tattoo?"

Her eyes flicker with something, but the very next second, it's gone, and I've lost whatever just crossed her mind. I wonder briefly what she's hiding. Surely, she knows about whatever it is Ares mentioned last night.

"I don't remember." She rises from the chair, ignoring my penetrating gaze, as she moves to the cooker, flicking it on and lighting the gas flame. "Did you want bacon and eggs? Or are you having cereal?"

"I'm not hungry." Sitting back, I lock my gaze on hers, silently pleading with her to just tell me what the hell is going on. "Ares mentioned something about our dads being friends."

"Why are you talking to that boy? He's trouble."

"He's the only one telling me about my family." This time I'm on my feet, frustration bubbling through me. "I have to get to class."

"Dahlia," Gran starts, but I'm not in the mood. I'd rather listen to Ares taunting me than to my gran hiding shit from me. Grabbing my backpack and keys, I head out the door, slamming it shut behind me. I immediately feel guilty for doing it, but I'm tired of being kept in the dark.

I deserve to know what secrets lie in my family.

Turning the engine of my car, I pull out onto the quiet street. Even though it's early, I will feel more comfortable at school than at home.

Home.

A strange place to me now. I grew up in a big city, living in the capital, with so many people who didn't know who I was. A stranger. For a moment, I wish I could go back there. This town is small, too small, and the fact that everyone seems to know each other's business is jarring.

I pull up to the school, killing the engine. I push open the door and grab my bag before heading toward the quad. The chilly morning air is evidence that we'll soon have snow on the ground—winter's coming.

A cold shiver trickles its way up my spine,

but it's not because of the weather. It's because I feel him as if he's magnetized to me, and the moment he's within range, I'm tugged toward him.

"There's the pretty flower." Ares' voice filters over the breeze as he nears me. He's alone this morning, and I wonder where his entourage is.

"What do you want?" I sigh, shouldering my backpack as I cross my arms in front of my chest. His gaze drops to my top briefly before flitting back to mine.

"I think we started on the wrong foot," he tells me.

I can't hide the frown on my face, confusion etched into every crease. "Oh? And what exactly is the right foot?"

"You asked me about your father last night," he tells me, and I nod. "I'll tell you. Everything." Ares lowers his voice, stepping up closer to me, offering me a whiff of the spicy cologne he's wearing. His dark hair hangs across his forehead, a dark strand falling into his left eye. His gaze is hardened, and by the way he's looking at me—hunger and danger emanate from his glare—I can't help but shiver.

"What's the catch?"

"Who says there's a catch?" he taunts, lifting his hand as he saunters around me, until he's right behind me. Heat cocoons me for a moment as both his hands land on my shoulders. His fingers squeeze my tense muscles. "You're in need of a rub down, flower," he murmurs in my ear, causing me to shiver as his warm breath fans over my cheek.

"What's the catch, Ares? I'm not here to play games."

"Oh, but games are so much fun," he whispers as his left hand grips my throat, holding me in place. The lump in my throat makes it difficult to swallow, and even though I'm sure he would love to hurt me, I know he won't. "See how easy it is…" His words trail off, and I shake my head.

"How easy what is?"

"You." One word, a slam dunk against my chest. "You're so needy for me, Dahlia. A flower calling to the bee." His voice is pure lust, but there's an underlying hint of venom just underneath the taunting whisper.

"Tell me," I say once I find the words. "Do you enjoy fucking with my head?"

"I'd much rather enjoy fucking your body—"

"Never going to happen," I bite out, interrupting him.

Ares chuckles, the low vibration in his chest makes the sound gravelly, and I can't stop my thighs from squeezing together. A few cars are pulling up, and I realize he has to stop this game now or students will see us.

"Do you want them to watch?" He hisses in my ear. "I do enjoy an audience."

"Fuck you, Ares."

"Mmmhmm, that's exactly what I'll do to you. Deep. Hard. Rough." With every enunciated word, his fingers press harder around my throat, making air difficult to pull in. My eyes flutter as my body turns hot and needy. He's right. He can read my body like a goddamned book.

"Let me go."

"Why? Aren't those pretty panties wet for me?" He taunts me as every word tickles the shell of my ear, but I can't answer. If I do, I'll admit I want him. I want this. I'm not sure what's wrong with me, but I can't find it in me to fight him. "I think the little flower wants her petals plucked by me."

"In your dreams."

"No, Dahlia." His voice hard, angry. "In yours."

Suddenly, he steps back, leaving me cold and shivering, and it has nothing to do with the weather. I spin on my heel to face him, taking in the satisfied smirk on his face.

"Are you happy now?"

"Quite. But it's not over." He smiles. "Soon, when you learn all about your precious dad, I'll be the one who you'll beg to make you forget."

I'm about to ask what he means when Rukaiya races up to me, not noticing the tension in the air between Ares and me.

"Later, my little flower."

Soon, he's far enough away, and I can breathe. When he's too close, it's as if my world is filled with Ares Lancaster, and my thoughts are racing. Rukaiya frowns as she takes us both in. "What the hell was that?"

"What?"

"You and Ares Lancaster eye fucking each other like nobody's watching." Rukaiya's voice is higher than I anticipated, causing a few students to glance our way.

"Would you keep your voice down," I bite out, tugging her along so we're not in direct line with everyone who can hear her. "We were not eye fucking each other."

"Oh? So, all that sexual tension that I felt as I walked up was my imagination?" Her golden brow arches as she regards me with a *don't fucking lie to me* look on her face.

"We were… It wasn't eye fucking." This time, I sigh, knowing she's right. I'm attracted to him. I can't deny it, but he's bad news.

"Come on." She pulls me along. "Time to get your ass in class, you can tell me all about Mr. Lancaster at lunch."

My feet follow along. But my mind is still on Ares and the way his hand gripped me masterfully. He's not old enough to hold that much power, control, or command.

And yet he does.

And he's lording it over me. One day at a time.

EIGHTEEN

Ares

I HAVEN'T STOPPED SMILING. I HAVEN'T STOPPED thinking about her and our little interaction this morning on the quad. And I certainly haven't been so hard for any female who's crossed my path. She's intoxicating, and I'm dying for another drink.

Strolling down the hallway, I find my father sauntering my way. He's finished his classes for the day, and I wonder if he's seen, Dahlia.

"Ares," he greets, stopping in front of me. "Tonight, the Sovereign want to meet. We have a little job for you and the rest of the new crowns." My father's eyes glint with excitement as he regards me.

"What time?"

"Seven," he responds as his gaze flickers behind me, and when I turn to see what's caught his attention, I find the pretty flower walking along the quad with her best friend. "Have you had any interaction with her yet?"

Do I tell him?

"Not yet," I answer, unsure of why I'm lying to my father, but I do. The lie flows without guilt, which sets me on edge.

His gaze darkens when he looks at me again, watching me as a hunter would its prey. "She can't find out about her father," he tells me earnestly.

"What? Why?" I thought the idea was to make her hurt, to see her break down when she learns who her father truly was. He lied to her all her life, and I can't wait to see her pretty face crumble with pain when she finds out.

"That's why we're meeting tonight. We have information on her father's partner," Dad says absentmindedly.

Shaking my head, I step closer to him, lowering my voice. "It doesn't change the fact that Patrick killed mom," I retort, as frustration burns through me like lava spewing from a volcano. Violence burns in my blood, and my knuckles itch, aching to hit something or someone.

"Listen to me," Abner grits through clenched teeth. "If you can't take an order, we will rethink your position in the society." Shock lances my chest. He's always been hard on Philipe and me, but the venom in his voice is nothing like I've ever heard before. The man before me is a stranger, not my father at all, but the man who runs a secret society of assholes.

"Fine." I turn to walk away, but his hand lands on my shoulder, and I'm certain he can feel the tension radiating through me. "I said fine."

He doesn't have to admonish me; I know he's warning me. It's time for me to let off some steam. When my father releases me, I make my way down the quad toward the parking lot where I spot Etienne.

"Hey," he greets as I near him.

"We have a meeting tonight."

He nods. "I know, we all got messages from an unknown number. Do you think it has to do with your pretty girl?"

"Apparently."

"You look like you need a time out," my best friend grins.

Just then, Tarian saunters up to us, stopping short when I pin a glare his way. "I need information," I tell him. "Hack everything you can break into; I want to know all there is to know about this Fergus asshole."

"Are you sure that's a good idea?"

"It's a fucking brilliant idea." Pulling my phone from my pocket, I tap out a message to Tar with the full name of the man in question. "I want it in an hour."

"Where are you going?" Both my friends question when I turn away from them, stalling me for only a moment before I smirk over my shoulder.

"To let off some steam." With a wink, I unlock my car and slip into the driver's seat. There's only one place that will ease the rage that's running through my veins right now.

Speeding through the streets, I turn up the volume on my stereo as 'Centuries' by Fall Out Boy screams at me through the speakers.

There's something about a hard rock song that gets me in the mood for what I'm about to do. My mind is still on Dahlia as I steer up the hill that takes me out of town and toward our neighboring shithole town.

Lakeside is nothing but a one-horse town. A dive bar, a few hundred homes, and a gym where I love to hang out when I'm in this crappy mood. I don't know many people here because they don't come to Tynewood.

The streets are bare, there's trash on the sidewalks, and the rundown building I'm heading toward beckons me like a light in the dark. When I pull into Billy's Gym, I kill the engine and exit the car.

Inside, I'm met with the stench of sweat and the grunts of men. Sitting in the center of the room is a ring, a square mat where two men are sparring like little girls swatting at bugs. No, this isn't what I want.

I make a beeline for the backdoor, which

I push open to find the space I'd been itching to enter. Two burly assholes are fighting like hound dogs, ripping their prey to shreds in the concrete fighting ring.

This is it.

War.

"Ares," Billy smirks when he notices me.

"Hey, B." I offer a hand, which he accepts and shakes in greeting. "Can I jump in?"

"You're one of my best," he tells me. "I'll get you in the next round."

"Good stuff." I settle back, watching the fight, while I tug off the T-shirt I'm wearing. My tattoo still stings every time I bump against it, but it's a reminder of what I'm walking into.

"Nice ink," Billy remarks, taking in the logo. It's one he knows far too well. I think it's something he'd much rather forget. "Dad make you get it already?"

"You know it." I grin. I've been fucked up drunk here so many times that I've found myself confessing things to Billy. I shouldn't have, but he's been good to me, better than my own father has been. Billy grew up in

Tynewood, his own father was a Crown, but when the old man died, Billy refused to step up. I never understood why, but he told me once that if I ever did become a Crown, I'd find out for myself.

"Be careful, Ares." Billy looks me over. "You're a good lad, I don't want you getting into that bullshit and losing yourself."

"I'll never lose myself," I admit, knowing it's true in my heart.

"Has he told you what he's done?" Billy asks before I have time to say anything more.

Shaking my head, I respond, "No. What do you mean?"

Silence weighs heavily between us. I can tell the man I've come to trust is at war with himself. He wants to tell me, but he's wary.

"Come on, B," I nudge him. "You've known me since I was seventeen. I can handle anything you throw at me."

He turns away, heading toward the counter behind us, and picks something up. Billy glances my way and hands me his phone. It's unlocked I take note of the Play icon waiting for me on the screen. There's a video waiting for me, and a cold, ominous shiver trickles its way down my spine.

"I don't know if I should show you this. It's not my story to tell, but…" He shakes his head and shrugs. "Here," he says, handing me headphones; I plug them in before hitting the large play button.

The images I'm met with turn my blood to lava, my stomach twists in knots at what I'm witnessing, and the dialogue that plays ensures I'm ready for a fight to the death.

Even though the object of my wrath isn't waiting in the ring tonight, I'll make sure soon enough, he will pay.

It's the last thing I see before I step into the ring and fight.

NINETEEN

Ares

I'M STILL BLEEDING WHEN I REACH THE DURAND mansion. My eye is burning, watering from impact, and I know, soon enough, it'll be swelling up. My lip tastes like metal each time my tongue swipes along the cuts. I fucked up the guy I was fighting, but he got a couple of shots in.

I stop at the gate and push the grey button, which buzzes the main house. It doesn't take long for the gates to open, and soon, I'm parked outside the large, ornate doors.

Etienne's mother is an interior designer with an eye for exquisite detail. She's redone their house more times than I've had sex, and that's a lot. But the moment I step into the foyer, I inhale the scent of home.

When my mother was killed, I was lost. And the only place that ever felt like home was the kitchen of Hilary Durand. Even though she didn't cook, the chef they'd hired used to feed me, making sure I'd had enough sustenance to make it to school and back again.

This will always be my home.

"What the fuck, man?" Etienne glares at me, and I know he's shocked at my appearance. After the video, I lost my shit. There's no doubt about it. I am volatile, more so than anyone ever thought I was.

"I needed something, man. I... I learned something that has finally broken my father's hold on me," I inform him, grabbing the beer he hands me. If I'm drinking, I may as well stay over, so I hang my car keys on the gold hook, which is secured against the inside of their kitchen door, and settle at the table that overlooks their vast garden.

"What happened?"

Shaking my head, I swig down the cold, bubbly liquid, knowing that if I get drunk before the meeting tonight, I'll probably kill my father.

"You can't hold out on me. We're in this together," he reminds me, but it's a lie. It wasn't his father in the video; it was mine. He has no clue how fucked up this truly is, and as much as I should tell him about it, I can't find the words.

"Not now."

Etienne glares at me for a long time before nodding. "There's a barbecue at the Calvert's," he tells me. "Want to head over before the meeting?"

"Yeah," I respond, swallowing the beer in a few long gulps. "I wonder if my little flower will be there."

"She's not a toy for you to play with, we need to tell her about her father."

"Fuck that," I tell him, still buzzing from adrenaline after having punched a man until he was practically passed out. Billy had to drag me out of the ring. "I'm the one running this, and she's mine." He's right, though. Etienne has this way of being right all the time, but this time… I don't care. Even as I think it, I know my conviction is slowly fading.

What my best friend doesn't know is that I enjoy playing with her, taunting her.

She's a toy. She's my fucking puppet.

Dahlia is here for me to amuse myself with, and I'm not about to walk away until I'm done with her. Before I saw that damning video, I wanted to kill Dahlia for what her father did, but now, all I want is to bend her over and claim her for myself. And that thought is what I'm at war with.

I don't *want* to want her. But there's no denying she's gotten under my skin. And now that I know the truth, I crave her more than ever.

"Everyone has a point in which they give in, this time… I've reached mine," I tell him, glancing up at my best friend who tips his head to the side. Silent code to let me know we need privacy.

He leaves the kitchen, and I stalk behind him as we head upstairs to Etienne's room on the second floor. The moment we reach it, I'm at the window. From here, I can see our house, and just behind it, through the trees on the hill, the old abandoned building my family owns.

The church that's been sitting there since before I was born. It's my sanctuary, and not in the way churches normally are; it's the place I can go wild, do things that could get me into trouble, but I no longer give a shit.

It's been a long time since I cared about anything.

Until Dahlia.

The thought appears in my mind out of nowhere, but I shake that shit off.

"What the fuck is going on with you?" His glare burns me, but even though I want to tell him about what's going on in my head, I can't. If I admit what I've been at war with, he'll only tell me to stop this game I'm playing.

"I don't know what you're talking about."

"Look, man, you know I'd do anything for you." Etienne's expression is filled with serious concern. "But this has to end sometime. She's not guilty; also, I have a feeling this girl could be good for you."

I can't help but laugh at that. *Good for me?*

"Really, man? You're turning into a little bitch talking to me about emotions and shit."

"I always knew you were a bastard, Ares, but I can see you like her. Why are you fighting it?"

"Stop giving me shit," I bite out. "I don't *like* anyone. Yeah, I admit I want to fuck her, but that's it."

"Is it?" He folds his arms across his chest as he stares at me, waiting for a reaction. I'm tempted to punch him, to fight him on this, but I don't. Instead, I hold my hands up in surrender.

"I'm not doing this with you right now."

"Why? Because I'm right?"

Shaking my head, I turn away from looking at him and instead focus my attention on the darkness beyond it. I wonder if I'm losing my mind, if I'm so broken, nothing jars me anymore.

"Look, I'm not fighting with you. I just hate seeing you act out when I can so fucking clearly see how this girl affects you."

"Yeah, because I hate her."

"Look me in the eye and tell me that?" Etienne's challenge has me spinning on my heel to glare at him. Meeting his curious gaze, I open my mouth to respond, but I can't find the words. "I thought so."

Shaking my head, I turn away, focusing on the window again, not wanting the judgmental stare of my best friend on me.

"We should go," I finally say, wanting to change the subject.

"Are we heading up to your house first, or do you want to just head to the barbecue? Tarian is already there."

The dark part of our triad, the third of the trio, is one of the more volatile. I may be named after the god of war, but Tarian, he's the fucking god of death.

I've seen him break men twice his size. Thankfully, our fathers have managed to sweep everything under the rug. Perhaps they shouldn't, but with our wealth and power, we're able to run the world without anybody noticing anything untoward.

"Yeah, let's see what he has up his sleeve."

I can't help but grin thinking of the Calvert household, I recall how one of my best friends has a sprawling estate to himself.

Tarian was orphaned the year he turned eighteen. Lucky bastard inherited everything. Billions. Along with a company, he now runs. Even though he works for my Dad, he doesn't have to. He's self-sufficient.

Slipping into the passenger seat, Etienne turns the engine on, peeling out of the driveway and drawing the attention of everyone in our vicinity as we make our way through this sleepy town.

I turn on the stereo. When the deep bass of the rapper, Savage's, 'Swing' blares through the speakers, I settle back and enjoy the vibrations that travel through me.

The streets are busy, but each time we pull up to a light, I notice people looking over at us. The music blaring from my window draws eyes to the car, and I revel in the attention. I guess Philipe was right, trouble and I are best friends, but that's just who I am.

When we reach the Calvert driveway, I

notice the gates are wide open with cars lining the path. We pass them, ignoring the common folk, as Etienne pulls to a stop in the space where I notice Tarian chatting up a stunning brunette. Killing the engine, along with the loud bass, I get out of the car and head toward him with Etienne hot on my heels.

It's the height of fall, and even though there's a chill in the air, it's like a wet dream out on Tarian's lawn. The fake green grass is filled with beauties settled under trees, giggling, and drinking. Large fires are blazing in pits situated in each area of the lawn.

"It's about time," Tarian tells me with a chuckle, shaking my hand first then Etienne's and pulling us both in for a slap on the back.

"I'm never late, just in time." I shrug then grin, eyeing up the beauty he's been talking to. "Hey, darlin'."

Tarian's eyes are luminous blue, it's as if you're looking through a window, especially when the sunlight hits them a certain way. He offers me a wink before turning to the beauty beside him. "This is one of the freshmen,

Rukaiya. I think you're acquainted with her friend, Dahlia," he tells me, gesturing to the one with the hair the color of charcoal.

Her body is hugged by a dark blue dress, which makes my cock wake up and take notice. She's an hourglass of perfection, her smooth porcelain skin makes my mouth water.

"Little flower, I didn't think you'd come out to play with us tonight," I remark, reaching for her hand, tugging her closer and pressing a kiss to her knuckles. "Looking stunning as always."

"And I see you're attempting to be charming, but failing as usual," she retorts hotly, which only makes me smirk. "We need to talk." When she says this, she leans in close, and I get a whiff of her perfume. It's not sweet like I thought it would be; instead, it's spicy, reminding me of cinnamon and nutmeg.

"Talk? Or is that code for something a little more intimate?" I ask her while offering a wink, which I know will only annoy her further.

"Don't change the subject, Ares. I'm

fucking tired of this back and forth." I'm shocked speechless at her fire. And the feisty little flower has me wanting to drag her into my car, drive her to my house, pin her to my bed, and make her scream my fucking name. She turns on her heel and heads toward a crowd of people standing around a table laden with red cups and bowls of chips.

"Tough crowd," I remark, staring at her curves. I cut a glance at Etienne, but he shrugs it off, and I'm even more confused. I haven't had anything delivered to her house, so this is news to me.

"Losing your touch?" Etienne grins, and I'm tempted to punch the fucker out, but he's lucky he's my best friend.

Her friend, Rukaiya, who witnessed the interaction grins sheepishly. "I'm sorry, Dahlia's a little…"

"Prickly?" I question.

She smiles then and nods slowly, and I wonder if she's afraid of saying anything negative about her friend.

"I'll get those thorns cut off soon." I wink,

slapping my best friends on the shoulders as I leave them and make my way to the woman who's got me by the balls.

I need to tell her what I've learned.

But I'm not sure how.

TWENTY

Dahlia

I FEEL HIM. SECONDS AFTER I WALK AWAY, HE'S behind me as I pick up the red plastic cup filled with bitter alcohol. I don't turn around; instead, I focus on my drink.

"Little flower," he murmurs in my ear, the warmth of his breath sending a shiver down my spine. He's fire and ice all wrapped up in a dark, broody package. His games, though, they need to stop. When I arrived home, there was a box in black wrapping on the step. I thought it was for my gran, but when I opened the small envelope, it was addressed to me.

"What happened to your face?" I ask, trying to keep my voice even. There are small scratches on his handsome face, and I wonder if he's been doing something illegal.

"Why? Do you really care, or are you trying to hide the way your body is trembling at my proximity?"

"This isn't a game, Ares," I tell him. I don't know why he wants to hurt me or what I've done to him. "If you can't be honest and tell me the truth, then I'll speak to your father."

His hands grip my hips, holding me in place. I can't move because even though there's anger searing through me, I can't ignore my body heating from his touch.

"I don't like threats, sweetheart," he whispers in my ear, allowing his lips to graze the lobe, sending another hot flush through every part of me. "And if you go near my father, he'll only have you removed from his town."

Spinning around, I meet those hazel eyes that have stolen every breath from me since the moment I looked into them. "You and your father have high regard for yourselves."

Ares glares, his teeth clenching, and I note how his jaw ticks with frustration. Perhaps I'm the first girl to ever fight back, maybe I'm the first girl to ever push him into a corner.

"My father, our parents, aren't who you think they are," he grits out. "But we can't talk here." Gently, his left hand trails up my torso toward my shoulder, and the moment it makes contact with my skin, goosebumps rise on every inch of my flesh. He grips me then, spinning me around, so our bodies are flush. The cup I'd been holding is taken from my hand. It's clear who's in charge here—and it sure as hell isn't me.

"I told you, you've walked into the wrong town," he murmurs; his voice low and seductive, as if he's trying to both scare and seduce me with one sentence. "But since you're here, and you're as stubborn as I am, I suppose you'll need to know what you're up against."

His words should scare me, but what he doesn't know is that I'm no longer afraid of what's going to happen. Anything Ares throws at me, I can handle.

"Take me to the church and tell me what I need to know. And when you're done, you leave me in peace." My retort earns me a smirk that makes my stomach bottom out. He's slowly getting under my skin, and it's so annoying. No, it's fucking frustrating.

I've never been so affected by anyone before. Yes, I've had crushes before, I even lost my virginity at prom, but this... It's as if electricity is shooting through every part of me. But it's not *only* attraction; it's the anger that wars with it. Ares makes me want him in ways I shouldn't.

"I'm not someone you can scare away, and I am certainly not someone you can fuck around with like a toy," I tell him, lifting my chin with confidence that only makes him grin. If I'm honest, the darkness I see in him intrigues me more than I'd care to admit. I want to see more of it, and it may be dangerous, but my body reacts to it in ways I can't decipher.

"You don't know who I am, who we are," he informs me with a glint of wickedness in his honey-colored eyes. "We're not playing kids' games here, flower," he warns. "This is bigger than both of us."

"You're so adamant you hate me, but I have a feeling you don't. Something tells me it's not me you're angry with but yourself."

"Oh?" he tips his head to the side, amusement dancing in his eyes. "And why would I be angry with myself?"

I want to tell him I know he wants me that I can see the desire that burns in his stare each time he looks at me, but I can't find the words.

He steps closer to me as if he's trying to mold himself into me. "You think I want you?" This time, his voice is tainted with a hint of a challenge, so I nod. "Mmm," he murmurs. "I do admit you make my dick hard if that's your idea—"

"Fuck you, Ares," I bite out in frustration, attempting to hide the blush on my cheeks and the way my nipples are hard against my bra. "If it's not me, then it's about my father."

"Fuck your father," he bites out, interrupting me once more. Rage dances wildly in his gaze, fire burning in those beautiful orbs. "Do you really think your asshole of a father is such a good man?" The sneer on his normally handsome face tells me this man knows my father far too well. And whatever it is he knows is not good.

"To me, he was." I'm adamant, which only earns me a smirk of derision. "Why? Take me to the church, I'll go willingly if you tell me." I tug free of his hold, needing to put as much space between us as I can. But I only get as far as the large wrought iron gates that stand open before I feel him following behind me. The night is much darker now, and the crowds have increased. He can't do anything to me since we're in public.

But something tells me he doesn't give a shit about who's watching. Like he said, this is his town. I reach my car and press the key fob before pulling open the door and slipping into the driver's seat, but before I can shut myself in, Ares is there.

His hand grips the door, holding it wide, so he can step closer to where I'm seated. He leans in, his left arm draped over the hood, and his fingers curled around the edge of the driver's door.

"I'll meet you there in thirty minutes, and if you're not there, I'll find you. And you don't want me to come running after you, Dahlia. You won't like the results." He bares his teeth; his anger is palpable.

Before I can respond, he slams the door so hard that I expect it to fall from its hinges. I watch him through the windshield as he saunters over to a girl beside his friend, pulls her into his arms, and whispers something in her ear.

My gut churns with anger and something I don't want to admit—jealousy.

By the time I pull up to my gran's house, I've calmed down, but my mind is reeling. Shoving open the door, I step out of the vehicle, shivering when the cool night air drifts over me, reminding me of the church.

My spine tingles and the hairs on the back of my neck stand on end when I feel someone watching me. My gaze darts around the darkened forest not far from where I'm parked. But I can't see anything in the shadows.

Rushing toward the house, I unlock

the door and enter its comfortable warmth, shutting myself inside. Closing my eyes, I pray the eerie feeling goes away sooner rather than later.

There's a lead weight in my gut from Ares' warning. And I know it has something to do with my father. Which only begs the question—what did Dad do to Ares' family?

It seems Ares and his friends run this town, and something tells me, this is only the start of him trying to scare me so that I'll leave. But Ares doesn't know I've had worse threats in my life, that I've been through worse, so his threats won't work.

I fight back.

And nothing he does can ever make me run.

The house is silent as I move through it. The living room is empty, and I wonder where Gran is. Perhaps she's out with friends playing Bingo or something. When I reach my bedroom, I settle on the edge of my bed. It's late, but I hit dial on Fergus's number. He knew my father for almost twenty years, perhaps he can explain what's going on.

"Dahlia, are you okay?" His voice is filled with worry, and I can hear the muffled sounds in the background. It sounds like a woman talking to him, which only makes me feel even more guilty. I shouldn't have bothered him.

"I…" My mouth goes dry when I hear the sound of glasses clinking, and I force my eyes to shut in frustration. "I'm fine, sorry to have bothered you, Fergus." I finally manage. I told Ares I didn't need my father, and Fergus is almost like a parent to me. If I told him what happened, he'd only drag me back to D.C. I have to figure out a way to get Ares to confess, on my own, what the fuck is going on.

"Dahlia." His concern is palpable. "Your father was a good friend, a partner, if something is going on, you need to tell me."

"Yeah, yeah, sorry to have bothered you so late, I just… I'm fine," I tell him, forcing a smile on my face in the hopes that he can hear it in my voice.

"Are you sure, Dahlia?"

"Yes, Fergus. I just wanted to let you know

I'm doing great." The lie burns my tongue, and he sighs.

"Good girl. If there was anything wrong…" His words taper off. "This town may be where your father grew up, but please be careful."

My brows furrow at his confession.

"What do you mean?" I question, shooting to my feet. I head to the window, shutting the curtains, and pray I'm hidden from the outside world.

"I just… I just don't like small towns," he tells me, but there's a hint of something in his tone, an inflection of fear, which sets my spine tingling once more.

"But that doesn't mean there's anything wrong. Right, Fergus?" I'm on the tips of my toes. I need to know the truth, but how can I tell if he's lying to me when I can't see his face.

"No, Dahlia. You're as tense as your mother used to be," he chuckles, shoving off the concern that's so clear in my tone. "Go to bed. I'll call you tomorrow."

I want to respond, but he's already hung up, and I'm sure he's with a woman, probably doing something I really don't want to think about what my best friend's father is doing.

Sighing, I place my phone on the nightstand before heading to the bathroom to splash water on my face. The mirror reflects my worried expression. I stare at the reflection before me: my makeup is non-existent, my lips are deep pink, and I have nothing on them. My wide eyes are the color of the sky, and my hair, which is loose down my shoulders, shimmers like the feathers of a raven.

Can I really trust Ares?

I don't know, but I'm going to take a chance and find out.

TWENTY-ONE

Ares

"I'M HEADING OUT," I TELL MY FRIENDS WHO are still drinking. I'm angry, too angry to get drunk and still keep a level head. Also, I promised Dahlia that I'd tell her. How the fuck am I meant to admit what I know?

"See you tomorrow," Etienne says from beside me. I know they both heard exactly what was said, so I don't respond.

"Do you think she knows what her father did?" Tarian voices the question that I've been wondering myself.

Shaking my head, I tell him, "I have a feeling Dahlia has no idea what her father is truly capable of." I fist bump them both before turning to walk away, but I'm not lucky enough to leave unscathed. Kelli stalks up to

244

me with a wicked smile on her face.

"Hey, boys," she grins, focusing her hungry gaze on Tarian. "Are you busy tonight?" She asks him, which causes me to glance at my best friend.

"Why? You looking to get your pussy fucked nice and hard? Or is it because you can't get Ares' dick, now you want mine?" He chuckles darkly, stalking toward her, causing that confident smirk of hers to falter.

"No, of course not." She lifts her chin in defiance. "I just wanted to know if you'd like to come to my place and help me study."

"Study?" This disbelieving question comes from Tarian.

"Well, more like a little get together." She twirls her dark hair around her finger as she pops her bubblegum. As I stare at her now, I wonder what I ever saw in Kelli. Yes, she's beautiful, but there's something extremely volatile simmering just below the surface.

"The Sovereign approves parties," I remind her. "And I don't recall hearing that either of us allowed it." She should know only me, Tarian, or Etienne can confirm if a party is happening. It's the rules of the town. If we don't agree with it, it doesn't happen. Simple as that.

She shrugs, her Botox lips pouting. "Well, I can always ask Philipe if he'll let me have one." Her words are poison to my already rage-filled blood.

One tiny step and I'm inches from her, gripping her neck. I walk her back until she hits the wall. She's pinned between me and the concrete. Her slim figure is no match for me. My fingers curl around her delicate throat, and the cuts on my fist are still burning like a motherfucker. When Dahlia asked about my bruises, I wanted to tell her, I craved her touch on the bloody cuts, because I know the moment we come into contact with each other, desire will take over.

Shaking my head of the thoughts of my flower, I focus on the girl in front of me. "Don't fuck with me, Kelli. I said no." I sneer down at her, my fingers tingling, wanting to squeeze as I take in her widening eyes. "If you go near my brother, I'll fucking end you," I bite out. "Do you understand me?"

"Why?" She challenges, causing me to squeeze just a little tighter and her eyes to slowly roll back in her head.

I lean in, my mouth at her ear, when I explain, "You and your filthy, needy cunt are not wanted anymore. I've let you go, Kelli. Remember the Sovereign doesn't like groupies." The only reason I uttered the word is because Kelli's foster brother is one of my underlings, and her father is one of the Crowns. Harding already hates me because I took her place at the table, but I don't give a shit. She knows better than to mess with the higher order.

And her foster brother is not a blood relation, so he can't take a seat at the table. We've been generous enough to allow him to run errands for us, anything more is unacceptable.

"But little miss orphan doesn't get told to leave you alone?" She hisses in my ear, and I know she's jealous of the attention I've given

Dahlia. What Kelli doesn't know is why. And she doesn't need to know.

I release her swiftly, causing her to keel over as she pulls in gasps of air before pinning me with an angry glare. "You're an asshole, Ares," she tells me, something I've known my whole life, and I don't give a shit. I rule this fucking town and school with the two men at my back, and nobody fucks with me.

"Get the fuck out of my face."

She obeys me because she needs to. No question, no disregard.

"You really know how to pick 'em, man," Tarian chuckles as he saunters toward me and hands me a red cup filled with beer. Shaking my head at him, I can't stop the grin that curls my lips. He's right, I really have a knack for finding the goddamned psychos.

"I'll see you later," Etienne tells me with a nod.

"Yeah, lover boy," I tease, earning me the middle finger as I stalk away, leaving my friends to deal with Kelli because, right now, I could kill her and not think anything of it.

In my car, I crank the stereo and peel out of the driveway, leaving smoke behind me as I head toward the church. I can't believe Dahlia suggested meeting there. After what I did to her, I didn't think she'd ever want to see that place again.

My phone blares through the speakers. With a quick glance at the screen, I tap the green button to answer. "Dad."

"Bring the girl to the lake house." Every word he utters turns my body cold, my blood freezing in my veins.

"What?" I choke out, pulling off the road before I get to the church. If she's already there, I don't want her to witness this conversation. He doesn't know what I learned, and I can't tell him over the phone.

"You heard me." Paper crinkles over the speaker, then shuffling, and then something that sounds faintly like a gun cocking. "Bring the Milton girl to the lake house, take her to the cellar, and wait for me."

"I don't understand."

"You will once you get there," he tells me.

There's no discussion; the line dies a second later, and I'm left staring at the screen. I'm not sure what the fuck the plan is, but I have an awful feeling about this.

Tapping out a message to Philipe, I hit send and give it time to be delivered. Once I see it's been read, immediately, three gray dots dance as he types his response. My heart is in my throat, thudding painfully.

I can't let Dad know I know the truth. And I can't tell Dahlia yet. If he wants to meet her then he has a plan, and if she knows what Billy showed me, she'll lose her shit in front of Abner Lancaster, and that will be the death of her. I don't know when I started giving a shit, but I do. I can't deny it anymore because as much as I want to hate Dahlia Milton, I can't. Because I want her.

At first, I wanted her to pay. I believed the lie I was fed, but now, the truth is a bitter taste on my tongue. Philipe's message comes through a second later.

Don't tell her anything. She needs to be

unaware of what her father did.

Shaking my head, I sigh. He doesn't know. Or perhaps my brother does know about our father's actions, and he's hiding it from me. Maybe he's played into this whole society for far too long, and he's in too deep.

I'm not sure what to say to him right now, but if he really has no clue, then I can't be the one to tell him. Abner made his bed, he needs to lie in it, breathing or not, dead or alive.

Turning the engine, I speed up the hill and come to a stop beside Dahlia's car, which is parked beside the building. She's still sitting in the driver's seat when I reach the door.

Her wide eyes lock on mine, those beautiful blue irises stare up at me as questions dance wildly in them, and for the first time since she arrived in town, I want to protect her rather than hurt her.

TWENTY-TWO

Dahlia

HE STARES DOWN AT ME, OPENING MY DOOR AND helping me out of the car. The way his fingers curl around my hand, the heat of his skin on mine, it all turns my body hot with desire. The way Ares is merely touching my hand is in no way the same as any time Josh was near me, or inside me.

"You came," Ares says, his voice low, a whisper of something warm lingers in his words as if affection is something he's giving me. I don't believe it. Not right now. He hasn't yet told me anything, and I'm still on edge from the last time I was here.

"I have to know the truth."

He nods. "You do. There are things your father kept from you." He helps me close the car door, before leading me into the abandoned building. Everything is exactly how I remember it. The cracked tiles, the altar, and with the full moon shining through the shattered windows, it casts an eerie, silvery light over the cold church.

Ares releases my hand, and I head to the small pew that's been pushed against the wall and perch myself against it. Even though I'm not comfortable, I cross my arms in front of my chest and wait.

"Your father grew up here," Ares speaks as he paces the floor. I watch him run his fingers through his unruly hair, and I wonder if he does it on purpose to give him a messy bedhead. "This town comes with its own set of rules; it comes with a society whose roots are firmly planted in the soil."

A laugh escapes my lips. "A secret society? That's such bullshit, Ares." I push off the pew and head for the door. "I thought you brought me here to tell me the truth, not to make up a lie about fantasies that you and your little friends hold."

I'm near the exit when his hand wraps around my arm, holding me hostage. "Listen to me, this isn't some made up story."

"Yeah? And what does your secret society do? Kill people?" Even at my nonchalance, fear skitters down my spine in a cold rush of anxiety.

"Yes." Just one word from the man before me makes every hair on my neck stand on end. My stomach twists with anxiety and lust, and I can't fight the attraction I have toward Ares.

I tug my arm from his hold, pinning him with a glare. "Don't lie to me."

"I'm not." There's brutal honesty in his words, in the deep gravel of his voice, and in his startling hazel eyes. Those two fucking words hold more truth than anything he's ever said, and that makes my stomach churn with unease. "All things done in the dark are hidden by the Sovereign."

"Don't talk in riddles."

Fire blazes in his eyes, making the honey color turn to gold. Ares leans in, his body engulfing mine, heat searing me from every inch of him that's pressed against me. Once again, I find myself against a wall with Ares Lancaster keeping me upright.

"If you're going to be flippant about this..." he smirks allowing his words to filter into nothing. His gaze drinks in every inch of my face. When his stare lands on my lips, it lingers for a moment, and hunger burns brighter than the confidence he exudes. "You're in danger, Dahlia," he tells me suddenly.

"Yeah? I've spent my life in danger. Do you think some little gang of boys are going to scare me off?" My words ignite something within him, and his hand trails up my arm quickly before gripping my neck. His fingers wrap around the column of my throat. He could easily squeeze and steal my breath, and I wonder briefly if he's contemplating it.

"You may think you know what we are, but you don't. Let's start with your precious dad," he sneers. "He became a cop after he left this town, acted as if he was too good for us."

"He wasn't like that. My father—"

"Was one of the Sovereign," Ares

interrupts. There's pure satisfaction on his face when he tells me this.

His confession stalls my words, causing my brows to furrow in confusion. "What? What do you mean?"

Gently, his thumb traces small circles along the pulse point in my neck. He tips his head to the side, watching the erratic movement of my heartbeat. He seems more intrigued by that than my question.

"My father and yours were close friends," he says then, "Your father wore one of the crowns, he was inked just like I am." For a moment, I'm confused, but Ares releases me and smiles when he tugs his shirt up and over his head, showing me the large emblem on his back. The dark ink crown along with a ribbon beneath and a date sits on his tanned skin.

I try to focus, but I can't stop my gaze from taking in every dip and peak of his toned body. He's slender, yet there's tightly packed muscle that makes me want to trace each contour with my tongue.

Get out of your head, Dahlia.

He turns to regard me again. "Enjoying the view?" Ares taunts. The corner of his mouth kicking up into a grin, gifting me a glint of pleasure in his intoxicating eyes.

"This isn't a joke. Tell me about my father."

"I told you he was one of us. He did things that were questionable in the eyes of the law. When he walked out of Tynewood, banished for turning in one of the brothers, he became a cop, married a pretty girl, and had a daughter."

"That's what you brought me out here to talk about?" I retort, frustration clear in my voice. "I know my father had a daughter. I know he was married. You're not exactly telling me anything new besides the fact that he had friends who didn't stick with him when he wanted a better life."

"A better life?" He chuckles darkly. "He would've had a far better life if he'd stuck to his vows, to the promises he made the Sovereign."

"Why?"

"We take care of our own."

"So that's why you hate him? Hate me?"

I lock my gaze on his, trying to gain answers to all the thousand and one questions racing through my head, but I can only voice one at a time.

Ares shakes his head. "I don't hate you at all, little flower. Not anymore," he murmurs, leaning in close, he feathers his lips over the shell of my ear, causing me to tremble with both tension and desire.

"What do you mean, not anymore?" This time, it's his turn to shiver when I whisper the words in his ear. The spicy cinnamon scent of his cologne wraps itself around me, and I wonder if I'll ever be able to wash it off or if I'll ever want to.

"I wish I could hurt you," Ares murmurs along my flesh, his lips burning every inch of skin as they trail a white hot path over the curve of my neck. His hand grips my hip, the other gripping my face, holding me steady. As if I'm merely a puppet for him to toy with.

"Why?"

"Because I like to see you filled with fear. I want to see you cry," he admits. "It makes me hard. It makes me want to steal your tears and drink them up."

"You get off on scaring girls?" I challenge, pressing my palms against his chest, needing air that's not filled with Ares, but he doesn't move.

"I get off on you," he confesses in a grave tone that has my wanton thighs squeezing together. "I want to see you lose all control. I want you to fight back, to claw at me while I make you scream my name. I can't stand the fact that I'm not meant to want you."

"Why are you not *meant* to want me?"

"Because your father did something to my family, something so atrocious, my father retaliated, and now we're even. And it doesn't matter what I do, I can never get a taste of you." His words cause more confusion than before. I thought I would get answers, but with every confession, all I have are more questions.

I'm not sure why I do it, why I lean up and allow my lips to touch his, but I do it anyway. Heat spears itself through me like a lightning bolt attacking my senses. Ares groans when his tongue darts out, licking at the seam of my mouth.

I want to open for him. I want to allow him inside. But I don't. It's a tease, a taunt to see how far he'll take it. I feel his mouth curve into a grin against mine.

"Teasing the predator isn't a good choice, little flower," he hisses through clenched teeth. Every word is like fuel sparking the fire inside me, stoking it, and making it burn brighter.

"I told you, I don't scare easily," I respond with my own gritted out promise. "What if you're the prey in this situation?"

His hands, strong and warm, grip my wrists, pinning them above my head against the cold, concrete wall. His hardness presses against my thigh when he pushes his body along mine, holding me hostage and in place.

"Is this what you want?" He questions, lowering his tone further until it's barely a whisper. But it doesn't matter because every word is a match, lighting me up. "You like it when I take it. Don't you, flower?"

"No."

"Oh?" He tips his head to the side, his eyes narrow regarding me as if he's trying to draw out the truth, but I don't give it to him. "So, if I put my hand in your panties right now, your pretty pussy won't be wet?"

Ares shoves his thigh between mine, the thick muscle pressing against my core, elicits a whimper of need to tumble freely from my lips. The sound makes him smile happily when he notes how much he actually does affect me.

"Mmm," he hums along my jaw, "I think my little flower is ready to be plucked." His mouth suckles on the sensitive flesh of my pulse point. The thrum is erratic and wild. His fingers dig into my wrists, hard and relentless.

I can't help but shiver when he pushes his leg against me once more, and there's no doubt that my panties are soaked.

"Tell me what happened between our families?" I ask, in hopes of him releasing me. Perhaps if I take his mind off the heat emanating between us, he'll focus and give me more than the tidbit of information he's already said.

"War, cruel fucking war," he bites out the words my gran used, which sets me on edge.

"What?"

"You heard me. What do you think comes with war, little flower?" He questions and the answer drops like a lead weight in my stomach. In this intimate position, I learn slowly what he's trying to say without uttering a word. I know what happened. The one thing I'd been dreading to hear.

With war comes death.

TWENTY-THREE
Dahlia

"My father wants to see you," he mutters when he pulls away from me. I'm still tingling from head to toe. A reprieve of cool air wafts through the cracked door, and Ares stares at me for a long while.

"Why?"

"I'm not sure." He shrugs, attempting a nonchalance that doesn't calm my nerves, and the knot that's forming in my stomach turns tighter with every passing second. "Look," he says, glancing at me, running his hand through his hair once more, causing the dark strands to stand in every direction. I find myself wanting to smile at the mussed style, but I focus on his words instead. "I believed a lot of things before you arrived; even when we first interacted, I thought…" He sighs, turning away from me, and I reach for him, wanting to know what's going on.

"Ares," his name is soft, a whisper of want, of confusion, and of need. "Please talk to me. I don't… I'm not sure why… Fuck."

He spins around, those caramel eyes meeting mine. "That word on your tongue is dangerous, little flower." This time, it's his turn to grin, *that* grin, the one that turns me inside out.

"Then give me honesty."

I'm met with a long sigh before he responds, "I don't know what he wants. If he knows that you're aware of your father's involvement in the Sovereign, I honestly have no idea what he'll do."

"Why did my father leave?" I ask, needing to know one more answer before I go with him. If he can't offer me the answer, then I'll ask his dad; Abner Lancaster has to tell me why my father would've walked out on something as serious as a vow he took.

"I told you," Ares responds, his hands

gripping my shoulders, holding me in place for a moment as he stares at me. "Come with me, let's go together. I'll explain to my father that you're not a threat to the Sovereign, and since your dad was a Crown, he has to show leniency."

"Leniency?" I squeak. Fear takes hold of me once more. The desire for Ares is gone, and I'm filled with trepidation as to what he could possibly mean.

"I won't let him hurt you."

Crossing my arms in front of me, I regard him before asking, "I thought that's your job?"

"It is." He awards me with a smile, a genuine one, that makes my heart do stupid things, like flip flop wildly in my chest.

"And how do I know you're not doing this because you're just obeying his request? What if you're still being a good little son running errands for a tyrant?"

Silence hits me hard when Ares doesn't respond. But it's not because I'm right, those honeyed orbs pierce through me, looking into my depths in an attempt to find my soul. But that's hidden away until I know I can fully trust him.

I may be attracted to the devil, but I'm not about to hand him something on a silver platter. "Unless you're afraid I'll walk out of here and make you do something you might regret."

"Don't fucking analyze me, you have no idea—"

"Then, fucking tell me!" I drop my hands to my sides, fisting them to keep from slapping him in frustration. My blood is hot, simmering in my veins. I'm angry and frustrated, and all I want to do is kiss him. My mind is a mess of emotions, and I don't know how to clear it up.

"My father had my mother killed," he tells me in a gravelly tone filled with rage and pain. "She didn't agree with his... methods, and when you disagree with Abner Lancaster, you pay the price."

"I'm so sorry." Stepping toward him, I reach for Ares' hand, the heat searing me the moment I make contact. His skin is smooth, warm, and his touch is gentle when he laces his fingers through mine. He lifts our hands, looking at the connection, and a small, wry smile dances on his lips.

"You didn't pull the trigger," he says, absentmindedly, but something in his tone when he says '*you*' makes my heart stall. Hazel eyes meet mine, the green flecks darkening considerably as he watches me. He's telling me the truth with a mere glance.

A lump forms in my throat, and I realize just why he hated me so much. He should. Even though it wasn't me who pulled the trigger, it was the man whose blood I share. The man whose DNA is racing through me at this very moment.

"It was my father. Wasn't it?"

Ares steps toward me, causing my back to hit the wall beside the door. Cold air swishes around us, and I shiver when he leans in, his mouth inches from mine. Electricity fills the air the moment his lips brush along mine. His breath comes in shallow wafts along with my own as if he's breathing me in and I him.

Back and forth, we inhale each other.

The minty breath of him mingled with the strawberry gloss that shines on my lips. We're so close, practically one person with two hearts and minds.

It's a scorching and volatile moment when he finally crashes his mouth to mine, and his tongue invades me like he's trying to steal every sound I make, along with the air from my lungs that I need to survive.

Can someone kill you with a kiss?

His body presses along mine, every inch of him against me. He's solid. I feel him, the hard ridges of his torso, the dips and valleys of his stomach against my softness. His one hand still holds onto mine as his other grips my long dark hair in a fist, tugging me this way and that so he can delve deeper into my warmth.

I can't think straight. His scent makes me drunk on him. I reach for him with my free hand, wrapping it around his neck, so I can pull him impossibly closer. That's when he releases me and grips my ass, lifting me against him and pinning me against cold concrete, but

I'm burning up.

A growl vibrates through his chest into mine. As much as he's taking from me, I'm stealing from him. A thief in the night, a vandal breaking down my walls, and I can't help but whimper his name.

When Ares finally pulls away, he's breathing heavily, his chest rising and falling against mine. My nipples are hard against him, and I wonder if he can feel what he does to me.

"If I slip my hand inside those panties right now," he hisses through clenched teeth. "Will you tell me to stop?"

I shake my head, unable to form words. The corner of his mouth tilts up as his hand snakes between us, his fingers finding my core over the tight yoga pants I'm wearing. He can feel my heat, how wet I am, and he can see the pleasure etched on my face when he presses against my clit.

"Ares."

"God, little flower, if you keep saying my name like that, I'll kidnap you and never come back," he promises, and for a moment, I want to ask him to do it. I want to beg him to steal me away and never return to this town where secrets and violence lie rampant among the shadowed streets.

"Take me to him," I finally mutter. "Take me to your father and let's finish this."

He stares at me for a long while before saying, "I can't promise he's not going to do something stupid."

"You'll be there." Ares nods. "I trust you."

"How can you?" He questions slowly, shaking his head. "What if I am lying? What if I'm using this"—he gestures between us, referencing our physical connection—"to worm my way into your heart and mind."

"I may be young, and I may not know much about your family, but there's one thing that's painfully clear," I tell him, feeling his fingers still on my ass, digging into the flesh. He's holding me so tightly against him, I'm sure if I move, he'll groan from the friction on his crotch.

"And what's that, little flower?" he

whispers along my cheek.

"The way our bodies fit, how you react to me, there's no way you can hurt me or have someone else hurt me." I half expect him to kiss me, to assure me I'm right because this can't be a game. *Can it?*

"You should never underestimate me," he promises before he releases one hand, keeping me in place with the other. He moves swiftly, reaching behind his back, and within a second, before I can fight him off, he brings a cloth to my face.

A squeal escapes my lips, and even though I manage to claw his neck with my right hand, my body slowly loses the fight. *I've made a mistake,* I think before my eyelids flutter closed.

TWENTY-FOUR

Ares

I MOVE QUICKLY. I SHOULDN'T HAVE DONE IT this way, but I have no other choice. If I take her to my father, he'll most certainly hurt her; I have no doubt about that. Lifting Dahlia in my arms, I move toward my car. Headlights meet me when I click the fob and unlock the vehicle.

Etienne and Tarian are quick to help me with her, slipping her into the passenger seat. Once she's secured with the seatbelt, I turn to my two best friends.

"This cannot get back to Abner or the Sovereign."

"Are you sure you want to put everything on the line for a girl?" This is Tarian, the levelheaded of our trio. He's more analytical with his thoughts, whereas I go on the passion that burns through me.

"I have to. I can't take her to the lake house, he'll kill her," I inform them both. The idea was to have her sleep through the short trip. Thankfully, when I called on my brothers, they were there for me, just like the Crowns should be.

"Will she be safe?" Etienne questions, and I nod.

"He's someone I trust. An old family contact that hates my father. He was a friend of my mother when she was still alive. I need time to figure out how to bring my father down. Billy will look after my girl."

"Your girl?" Etienne raises a brow at me, a knowing smirk playing on his lips. He called it the moment I laid eyes on her.

"I no longer have a choice."

"Then consider her a Crown." Both of them smile, gripping my shoulder and offering a reassuring squeeze. "You better get out of here, or he'll find out about this plan before you reach the next town, if you need the plane, it is on standby."

"Once I get to Billy's I'll decide if we fly out of town, or we stay put. I need to wait until Dahlia wakes up. I want to finish this, my father needs to pay, but if she wants to run, I'll go with her."

Both men look at me and nod. We're no longer the teenagers that started out as friends, we're men who have become a brotherhood, and I would do anything for them, and I know they'd do anything for me.

"We're waiting on your order," Tarian informs me.

"Okay." Giving them a mock salute, I make my way around the car to the driver's side and slip in. The moment the engine purrs to life, I'm peeling out of the parking spot and down to the road out of town. It's the second time today that I'll be leaving the place I grew up in.

Once my mother was murdered, I closed myself off to everything. Nothing could make me leave here. I waited for Milton to return; instead, his daughter came for me. To free me from the shitshow my life had become.

I didn't notice it at first, but she lit a fire that burned in my gut. I hated her, I was angry for what her father had done, but then the video opened my eyes. Lies twisted in my chest, every word my father had told me was nothing more than fabricated bullshit.

Lights in the distance flicker and I know we're almost out of Tynewood, which will get us closer to our destination without Abner finding us. Being a Sovereign, I can make it seem as if I've disappeared for however long I need. Etienne and Tarian will be the only people who know where I am.

The problem is, Dahlia needs to go to school. She can't disappear. She has a life, and because she has her gran, her friend, Rukaiya, and her friend's father, Fergus, who's a cop— one who won't stop until he's uncovered the truth, which can't happen. Ever.

And for the first time since my plan came to fruition in my mind, I feel guilty stealing the pretty little flower.

My phone beeps as I near Billy's house. A

message from Tarian.

All set. Her gran thinks she's staying with Fergus and his daughter for a couple of days since it's a long weekend. You have forty-eight hours, man, don't fuck this up.

I don't respond because I know the moment I do, my phone will be tracked, so I turn off the signal. The drive here was the most torturous one I would ever make. The phone ringing drags me from my thoughts as I tap the green button.

"Yeah?"

"Where are you?"

"Almost there," I tell him quickly. I didn't have a choice, and I hope she'll forgive me. I don't know what's happened to the anger I felt toward her, perhaps it's learning who my father truly is.

"We're waiting."

I hang up and focus on the road. I need a fucking drink, but getting to the house is my main priority right now. The car swerves through the dark streets, and I can't help but glance at the passenger seat. Dahlia has been out of it for an hour. I have ten missed calls from Abner Lancaster, but I ignore the niggling in my gut that tells me the moment he finds us, we'll be dead.

I should've been at the lake house an hour ago.

He knows.

Of course, he knows. But the more I can put him off, the better. Each time lights appear in the rearview mirror, my heart thuds against my ribs. Before us, the estate comes into view, and I realize this wasn't what I should've done, but I had no other choice.

The ornate gates appear as we inch closer to the mansion that sits on a vast plane of land. I should've taken her to the city, where she can disappear, but instead, I called one man I know my father won't fuck with.

When I come to a stop outside the door, he's already outside waiting for me. Even though he runs a gym in town where I tend to spend most of my nights fighting, Billy has a mansion from family money.

"She still passed out?" He asks, gesturing to the passenger seat.

"Yeah, I think she'll be out for another thirty minutes or so," I inform him as I pull open the door and scoop her into my arms. She's definitely out because she's leaning into me as if I'm her savior. "He's been calling me non-stop."

"You sure you want to cross your old man?"

Pinning Billy with a glare, I nod. "He lied to me. Killed my mother."

"But you don't know the circumst—"

"Fuck the circumstances! He had a choice, now I'm making mine." I follow the old man into the house, and he leads us up the staircase and down a long, dimly lit hallway. Billy pushes open a bedroom door, and when I step inside, I can't help but breathe easy.

The space is beautifully furnished. It's spacious with a large four poster bed. A window overlooks what I'm guessing to be the garden. Opposite the entrance is another door, which looks like it leads into a bathroom.

"She'll be comfortable. You and I need to talk."

I nod, setting Dahlia on the mattress, before pulling a blanket over her. Once she's settled, I watch as Billy locks her in.

"Is that necessary?"

He glances my way before nodding. "If she gets out and doesn't know where she is, she's going to lose her shit. I'd rather she smashes the room to pieces than my house when she finds out what you did to her." He's right. The moment she wakes up, Dahlia will be like a firecracker going off.

I think of the video, of knowing my father was the one who orchestrated my mother's murder, banking on me seeing Patrick pull the trigger. He threatened Dahlia's life once before, when she was only a teenager, forcing her father's hand. He knew about her long before she walked into Tynewood.

It wasn't the Sovereign who didn't want women at the table; it was Abner Lancaster who allowed the need for absolute power to take over and rule him. He got hungry and vicious, and it's time that came to an end.

Even though I wanted to be by Dahlia's side the moment her eyes open, I need time to talk to the man who's giving me refuge, as well as helping me plan how to take my father down.

One way or another, he'll pay for what he's done.

It's funny how things can change overnight. Twenty-four hours ago, I was ready to make Dahlia's life hell, now I'm the one saving her from my father's wrath.

War is coming.

And it's definitely going to be fatal.

TWENTY-FIVE

Dahlia

PAIN SHOOTS THROUGH MY HEAD WHEN I OPEN my eyes, causing me to groan. A bitter taste lingers in my mouth, but there's a scent of flowers—lilies maybe—that assaults my senses.

Pushing off the comfortable bed, I fight the urge to puke. My head spins. Or is it the room that's spinning? I'm not sure, but I'm not at all steady on my feet. Gripping the mattress, I hold on in an attempt to calm the surge of saliva in my mouth and the way all the furniture seems as if it's trying to attack me.

Once the feeling passes, I right myself and head to the door. Tugging on the knob, I twist and pull, but nothing gives way. With both hands, I slam my fists on the wood, screaming for someone to let me out.

I wait for a moment before doing it again and again until my throat is burning from the effort. Silence greets me, responding with nothing more than the promise that Ares drugged me, kidnapped me, and brought me to…

I glance around the room, taking in the expensive furniture, the silk curtains, and plush carpet. There's a door cracked on the other side of the room, probably a bathroom, but I don't move toward it.

My heart catapults in my chest when I hear a key in the door behind me. Spinning on my heel, I note that my shoes are off. Every nerve in my body is alight with fear and anxiety as I watch the gold doorknob twist, and when I'm met with familiar hazel eyes, I leap at Ares.

I beat my fists on his chest, his body slumping backward at my attack, but he quickly rights his footing. Ares grips my arms lifts me from the floor, and walks me back into the bedroom, kicking the door shut.

"What the fuck did you do to me?" I screech at him.

His response is merely a grimace at the sound of my voice, the high pitch of the words that spill free from my lips.

I continue my attack. "You're a fucking asshole. You fucking drugged me. You're going to kill me. Aren't you? Why the fuck—"

Suddenly, I'm on the mattress, bouncing from being dropped without a care in the world. This man, this beautiful fucked up man stands before me, arms crossed as he regards me as if I'm annoying him.

"If you continue acting like a child, I'll treat you like one."

"Fuck you, Ares. Take me to your father. I want this over with." I'm on my feet, inches from him. "You promised to give me the truth, and when you do, you kidnap me. People will look for me. You're not getting away with this."

Ares sighs, turning away from me, and that's when I lose all control and leap onto his back. He catches me easily as if he was waiting for me to do it. His hands on my legs make my body react in a way I hate. I don't want to want him. I hate that he has this control over me.

"Put me the fuck down."

He does, causing me to stumble backward. Ares turns his hard gaze on me. "Are you going to listen to me? Or lose your shit when I'm trying to save your life?"

His words have their desired effect, and I still, staring at him as if he's speaking another language. "What?"

I watch him move across the room, settling in the window seat, which I didn't even notice was there. He's dressed in jeans, a black T-shirt, and sneakers. He looks so relaxed as if this is all normal.

"I brought you to a friend's house who I trust. We're just outside Tynewood. Your grandmother thinks you're spending the weekend at Rukaiya's place."

"How would she—" I stall my words. I feel my pockets for my phone, but quickly realize that it's gone. "You stole my phone?"

"I borrowed it. Nothing is stolen," he tells me, pinning me with a frustrated glare. "My father wants to hurt you. I can't let that happen."

"Why? Because you want to hurt me?"

The corners of his mouth twitch and I know he wants to smile. The darkness that dances in his expression is evidence enough of how much he'd enjoy seeing me cry and beg for mercy, and I know it's something he still thinks about.

"I have to be honest," he says, rising from the chair and stalking toward me, as he regards me with an almost playful smile. "I do love seeing those wide eyes of yours fill with fear, yearning, and want."

His body is inches from mine, burning hot while I'm shivering against the wooden pole of the four-poster bed. My back is flush with the cool object, and the heat searing me from Ares is turning my mind over a million times a minute.

"The way your lips part," he murmurs. "How your breath comes in short warm spurts, and those cheeks of yours," he runs his knuckles over my face, over the heated flesh where I know embarrassment is burning me up, "how they turn bright red when you're turned on."

"I'm not turned on."

"Really? Because I know you like the idea of being with the bad boy." He smiles. "You like the danger." Ares presses his body against mine. Even though I'm shorter than him, I feel him, every inch of him. His index finger tilts my head, so our gaze is locked. "Tell me, little flower." There's an urgency in his tone as if he's really intrigued by the idea of me wanting him.

"Maybe," I find my voice. "Maybe, I'm just playing you like you enjoy toying with me." I roll my hips, earning me a low, feral groan from the man in front of me. "Or perhaps, I'm just not that into you, Ares Lancaster. I could be here for my own life for my family's name." This time, I smile at him. "Maybe your father has already paid me to make you fall for me and then twist that thing you call a heart in your chest until it's as ugly as his."

"What?" He rears back as if I'd slapped him viciously. My heart and mind whirl with the pain etched in his eyes. *Does Ares really like me?*

"Are you shocked that I can play this game as well as you can?"

As if a match had been struck, Ares' eyes light up with a fire that steals my breath, and soon, I'm pinned by my neck against the hardwood behind me, his fingers wrapped around my throat.

"Tell me," he bites out. "Tell me you're fucking with me. Because if you're working for Abner, I won't think twice about killing you." Fury laces his words.

"Ares." A man's voice startles us both, and quickly, the breath-thieving hand is gone, and I'm gasping for air. "Get ready, the plan is in place."

As if a puppet on a string, Ares moves quickly, leaving me with an older man I've never seen before. He's graying at the temples, and the salt and pepper strands that offer up a full head of hair glint as he moves closer.

He has a dark beard and luminous green eyes. Familiar eyes. I can't quite place where I've seen him before, or why he seems so familiar, but when he nears me, I can't help but cower.

"Don't mess with Ares. He may be young, but he's volatile and strong, and when he loses focus, he could hurt you."

"I'm not afraid of anyone," I bite out, unsure of where my strength comes from.

He smiles. "You're a strong girl." Silence hangs between us, but I can tell he wants to say something more. "You're going to be good for him."

"What makes you think I want him?"

"The fire between you two is palpable. And I've never seen him so intrigued by someone, and for him to go against his father, that's something I never thought I'd see. Even after all the things Abner has done."

"Abner is a monster."

The man nods in agreement. "He is. I've known him my whole life. And when I walked away, it was the best thing I'd ever done."

"So why does Ares stay?"

I watch as he considers my question: his brows furrow, his lips tilt to one side, pursing in concentration, and I wonder briefly if he's trying to find words that won't incriminate the man who's etched himself into my life and my body.

"Ares has struggled all his life, and it's not my place to tell you the secrets of the Lancasters, but maybe if you let Ares in, he'll trust you enough to let you get closer than anyone ever has."

"You think he likes me?"

"He would never have done this for someone who wasn't a Crown." The older man offers a small salute, and I'm confused at what he means. The Crowns are who Ares mentioned at the church. My father was one. But Ares hates him, so he can't mean him. But does that make me one? "I better get ready for tonight. It's time the truth reveals itself." He turns and walks to the door, and all the questions I have for him are sitting on the tip of my tongue.

Only one frees itself. "Did you know my father? He was a Crown, right?" I want to run to the old man, to ask him to stay so he can confess everything, but I don't. Instead, I wait for him to answer me.

The stranger doesn't look at me, but I notice how his shoulders tense. His hand on the doorknob tightens, his knuckles turning white.

"I did. He was a good man, and yes, he was a Crown. Stay here for now; tonight, we'll have a dinner, and all the secrets will be revealed."

Then I'm left alone with my thoughts. I don't know what to do. How I'm meant to stay here while Ares runs around putting himself in danger for me. I'm not some weak girl who can't fend for herself.

I crawl onto the bed and close my eyes, wondering just what is going to happen tonight.

A dinner?

Will Abner be here?

Is Ares going to hand me over like a sacrifice?

If he does, I'll fight. I'll never stop fighting because my father taught me to be strong, and now is the time to make him proud.

Why did you do it, Dad? Why did you kill a woman for no reason?

TWENTY-SIX
Dahlia

I STARTLE AWAKE TO THE CLICKING OF THE LOCK on the bedroom door. Making my way toward it, I find it unlocked. When I twist the knob, it opens, allowing me to wander down the dimly lit hallway.

My stomach rumbles, and I realize I haven't eaten anything all day. Sleep stole me, and the exhaustion of everything that's happened kept me under the covers.

Everything is lit in a soft, yellow light as I make my way toward the dark wooden door where the loud sounds of rock band In This Moment scream through the wood with their song, *'Sick Like Me.'* I lean against the jamb, listening to the song before I'm met with silence once more.

It's time to talk to Ares.

When I stumble into the bedroom, my glance lifts to the bed, and there, in all his beautifully toned glory, is Ares, in nothing but a white cotton sheet covering his groin. My mouth dries, my tongue feels as if it's three times its size, and my throat is filled with words that won't come.

I lift my gaze, further struggling to drag it away from the smooth planes of his body and meet those amusement and lust filled hazel eyes. He knows I can't look away, and I know it, too.

I never thought I'd see him naked, let alone without a girl keeping him company, doing something I'd rather not think about, but he's alone.

"You just going to stand there, gawking?" He arches a brow, his gaze lingering on mine then slowly trailing a white-hot path down every inch of my clothes that suddenly feel too warm for the heat that's filling the room.

"I... I should go," I finally utter, but there's no conviction in my voice.

"You should stay, sit awhile." He smirks. "I mean, don't you want to see what's under the sheet?" His question causes my face to flush, the heat spreading from my cheeks to my chest, and I know the bastard can see it. His hand grips his hardness under the material and slowly moves as if he's trying to hypnotize me.

"You're... I'm not working for your father." I don't know how else to make him believe me. He shifts, and I can see the bulge that's so prominent under the material, causing me to avert my gaze away from the way the sheet moves when he does. "I just wanted you to know. But I need to leave. It's time I went home, found Abner to finish this."

"Oh?" That dark brow arches once more, and his mouth kicks into a wolfish grin. "And what makes you think I'll *let* you walk away?"

"You've made it very clear I'm an annoyance to you," I retort while crossing my arms in front of my chest. "Why not let me leave and sort things out with your father directly?"

"Because you're *my* annoyance to deal with," he tells me as if it should all make sense to me. But it doesn't. None of this makes any sense because even though he doesn't want me in his life, which he's made clear, why not just take me to his dad and get this over with. I should go. This is pointless because Ares is stubborn.

So why am I just standing here?

"I'm not staying," I inform him, before turning to walk away. I'm four steps away from his door, when a hand grips me, so harshly, I almost stumble, but strong arms wrap around my midsection before I'm hauled backward, farther into the bedroom.

The door is kicked shut, and I'm released. I pivot, my gaze landing on Ares in nothing but the mischievous grin on his handsome face. His body is bare of any clothes, and I can't stop my eyes from dropping to the thick cock that's jutting from his hips.

I can feel my cheeks heat. The flush of them apparent, and I wonder if he can see the pink hue trailing from my face down to my chest.

"What the fuck are you doing?" I grit through clenched teeth. I want to turn and leave the room, but when I lift my eyes, I find his shining with mischief.

"Like I said, little flower, you're not leaving."

His hand lands on the wall behind me; he's once again caged me in, but I don't fight it. My body aches low in my stomach, and I allow him to run his knuckles over my jaw. His eyes are fire, burning into me. Ares lowers his mouth, brushing full lips against my trembling ones.

When he finally steals my breath, I arch into him, causing him to growl. The animalistic sound is low and feral. His hands roam their way to my hips, gripping me so hard that I'm certain he's bruising me, marking me as his.

I'm his toy, and there's nothing I can do about it. Our tongues duel like warriors in war, slashing against each other in violent, passionate licks. A dance of desire laced with the danger of violence.

Ares lifts me against him, carrying me to the bed and laying me down far too gently. But that doesn't last long, because the moment he opens his fire-laden eyes, I'm scorched beyond repair. He practically rips my yoga pants from my body. My panties are next to go, and soon, I'm naked, taking note of my tank top that's been discarded in a pile of torn material.

I take in every inch of him. Tightly packed, which makes me lick my lips as toned muscles tense and release. His abs are defined to peaks and valleys of beautiful flesh. A deep V points toward a thick cock that's hard and shimmering with his arousal.

When I finally meet his gaze, it's drenched in absolute power. A man so young wields power me with one single glance.

"Are you sure you want to do this?" He arches a brow as if he's challenging me, and I'm about to fall apart. But I don't.

Keeping my composure, the bare minimum that's there, I smile. "Give me your worst." The taunt makes the corner of his mouth kick up.

He nudges between my thighs and then his mouth attacks me with a vengeance: my neck, my shoulders, and when he reaches my breasts, his mouth latches on to one peaked bud, suckling it into his mouth.

My hands tangle in his dark strands, tugging him closer, needing more of him. My back arches and my toes curl when his teeth graze along my nipple, sending jolts of desire and pleasure shooting through me like an electric spark coming to life.

Hungry lips move lower, over my belly button, until he stops at the juncture between my thighs. I'm already trembling and needy. All I want is him inside me, but he doesn't move.

His breath is warm as it whispers over my hot core, causing me to tremble under him. He's toying with my body, a master at the pleasure he's bestowing on me, and I can't stop whimpering for more. With a long, slow, torturous lick, he tastes me, and I can't stop myself from crying out his name.

"That's what I like to hear," he tells me.

"Now remember, that's the name you'll be screaming when you come." That's my only warning before he crashes his mouth down on me and licks, laves, and sucks on my clit until stars blind me behind my shut eyelids.

I can't focus. My heart is thrumming, my stomach slowly tightens with the impending orgasm. Ares sinks two fingers into me, gently, slowly fucking me at a pace that's turning my body inside out. He works me into a frenzy, and with every moan, he moves faster. Soon, I'm arching off the bed as his hand moves at a violent pace.

I raise my hips to meet his mouth, again and again. A low chuckle vibrates from his lips to mine. "That's it, my little flower, fall apart for me." His voice is laced with thick desire as I tug his face against me. My toes curl into the mattress when Ares dips his fingers so deep inside me I see stars, as he sends me tipping over the edge of madness.

The second I fall, I scream his name loudly, making my throat burn. And it's in that moment that I realize that Ares has just won this war, and I'm a bloodied casualty at his feet.

TWENTY-SEVEN

Ares

SHE'S PLIABLE UNDER ME. MOVING OVER Dahlia's sweet body, I lean on my elbows, my cock nudging her wet pussy, and I'm tempted to slip inside her without a word. But I watch her for a moment as her eyes flutter.

Her face is a picture of pleasure.

When she looks at me, I can tell there are a million questions dancing in her stare, but there's no time for answers. Gripping my cock, I line myself with her entrance.

"One more chance, little flower. Tell me no, and I'll stop," I breathe the words along her neck, taunting the smooth flesh with my lips. I meet her gaze, waiting for her to stop me. Her mouth falls open as the tip of my cock nudges her entrance. "Because the moment you let me inside you," I tease her with my dick before continuing, "that means you're mine." It's a warning.

"Wasn't I always yours?" She sasses me, and that's all the invitation I need. Driving my hips toward her, I'm instantly balls deep inside her. She's so fucking tight; she feels like a virgin wrapped around my dick, and pleasure heats my blood to the point of pain.

"You're going to make me lose control," I manage to grit out through clenched teeth. I can't come yet; I need to make this good for her, even though there's no way I'm going to last long.

My mouth finds hers, our tongues darting out, dueling with each other. A fight for dominance, a war of need, and desire. Her soft lips are warm against mine, and there's a sweetness to her taste, but I know there's a darkness inside her under that sugary goodness.

When I pull away and roll my hips, I can't stop the stupid grin on my face when her back arches from the mattress and her eyes roll back in her head. I mimic the move a second and third time, making her claw my shoulders as she whimpers my name.

My fucking name.

From the first time I saw her, I knew I wanted her, but this is something out of this fucking world. Her tits are just more than a handful, and I latch onto a rosy nipple, sucking it into my mouth. My teeth graze along the bud, earning me another sexy moan.

My cock hardens even further, and I plunge myself so deep inside her that we both groan as pleasure zips through us.

"Please, Ares, please," she begs, pleading with me for something. Our gazes lock for a long, intense moment. The room is filled with the smell of sex. Her body's attached to mine like we're one person, no longer separated.

This can't last long. It won't. Because the moment she knows my plan, she'll run.

Ignoring the nagging in my mind, I lean in, my mouth sucking the soft skin of her neck, and I bite down hard, earning me nails tearing through skin as her cunt convulses wildly at the act.

I do it again and again, and I know I'm leaving a mark. My mark. When I lift my head, there's a soft pinkish red bruise forming on her pale flesh. Dahlia lifts her hips, and I realize I've stilled all movement, I'm in awe of her.

"Fuck me, Ares," she pleads, and I obey. Pinning her to the mattress, I lean up on one elbow and grip her bruised neck with my free hand and squeeze. Her eyes widen: fear, lust, and anxiety swim in those blue eyes, and I know this is what she needs.

My hips thrust wildly, needing to be inside her more than my next breath. Her body pulses around my shaft, tight and warm, causing me to groan as feral pleasure burns in my veins.

Each movement is like an aphrodisiac. Her hands tangle in my hair, pulling me toward her, and I offer her the kiss that steals every sound she makes and every breath she attempts to pull in.

"Come on my dick, little flower, I want to feel you milk me," I whisper in her ear before

I reach between us and circle her clit, which makes her walls suck me in deeper.

"Oh, oh, oh, fuck," she whimpers as her head falls back on the mattress, and her body arches so beautifully that I'm entranced by her.

Pleasure skitters down my spine, my balls tighten, and I empty myself inside her. Jolts of heat wash over me as I shut my eyes for a moment and live in this blissful moment. It's the first and last time I'll have her like this, and I bask in it for a moment.

I don't want to face reality.

I can't let her go.

But I know it's the only way.

The moment I open my eyes, I find myself alone in bed. No evidence of Dahlia being here beside me. I know it was real because her scent is all over me. And that only makes me want her again.

Music filters from somewhere in the

house, and suddenly, my bedroom door is shoved open as my two best friends saunter inside. Etienne and Tarian are both dressed in their finest custom cut black tuxedos with white button ups and black bowties.

It's almost time for the party, and I wonder if Dahlia knows about it. If she knows who will be here and what we're risking bringing the asshole here.

"Yo, get your ass out of bed and put some clothes on."

Rolling my eyes at Tarian, I get up, with no modesty and turn toward them. "Where's Dahlia?"

"God, man, put your junk away," Etienne grumbles. "I don't need to see that shit before the party."

"Why?" I taunt. "Going to be thinking of me while you're balls deep inside some pretty girl?" I grab my dick to make my point, causing him to shake his head in frustration at me. My body's one thing I've never been worried about showing off in public, and tonight, that's going to come across loud and clear when my father sees what I have planned.

"Fuck off, get your ass downstairs. B said he has Dahlia getting ready. He hasn't told her about your dad," Etienne tells me. I can see the trepidation in his eyes. He knows this could go either way: with me or Dahlia dead.

Casualties of war are to be expected. But I won't let him hurt her. There's no way he'll get close enough to her to do anything because we'll stop him before he has a chance. The plan is in place, he's outnumbered, and once he gets here, I'll tell him what the Sovereign will stand for in the future.

"Is Philipe coming as well?"

Tarian nods. "He's coming. The asshole knows she's here; I think we may have trouble with your brother, Ares." The warning doesn't sit well with me. I thought for once Philipe would see it my way. That he'd support me as the future of the society. But my father's chokehold on us runs deep.

"Fine, leave me. I'll get ready."

Once I'm alone, I head into the attached bathroom and turn on the taps. I wanted this to go smoothly, but anxiety twists in my gut. I'm about to step under the spray when I hear my phone vibrating on the nightstand.

I grab it, swiping the screen. "Yeah?"

"Brother," Philipe greets me. "I know what you're doing, or what you're trying to do. Are you going to choose a girl over your own blood?"

"You know what, for once, I wish you would trust me. I know I've never been the easiest person to be around, but believe me, when I say, I'm not doing this to break our family up. And I don't need your help."

"Like fuck, you don't. Tell me what you're doing, Ares," he urges, and as the steam wafts from the bathroom into the bedroom, I tell him the one thing I haven't yet said out loud.

"Dad had mom killed."

I hang up before he can respond and make my way into the bathroom to step into the shower. The water is scalding, burning me from the outside in. For the first time in years, I feel like I know what I'm doing. I feel the nervous energy that normally comes before a fight, and it makes me itch to get down there and show my father I'm more man than he will ever be.

I want him to see how much he's underestimated me. Tonight, the Sovereign may fall, but the brotherhood will always be there. Shutting off the taps, I take a long, deep, and cleansing breath. Then I make my way to the closet and get ready.

It's time to end the war.

TWENTY-EIGHT
Dahlia

THE MIRROR REFLECTS A GIRL I DON'T RECOGNIZE.

It's not the expensive, white satin, cowlneck dress Ares got me for the evening, it's not even the jewelry I'm wearing. It's him. He's gotten into my heart, into my very soul, and I can see the way my eyes shine with emotion.

I've fallen down the dark hole alongside Ares, and I don't know what will happen if I have to walk away from him. If I'm forced to leave, I don't think I can go on knowing love is possible and not have it in my life.

Because I do.

I've fallen for him.

And for a moment, I miss my best friend. Rukaiya would listen to me complain about

310

how stupid my heart is for falling for a man like Ares Lancaster.

As I think his name, the bedroom door slides open behind me. When I glance up, looking in the mirror, I find Ares dressed in a suit with a white shirt, black tie, and shiny black shoes. A picture of perfection. He nears me, and instantly, my body heats when I remember what we did only hours ago.

I recall every moment of how he felt inside me, how his mouth and fingers brought me pleasure I never knew before. With a soft kiss, Ares makes me shiver as he cocoons me from behind. He's a head taller than me, and I have to tilt my face ever so slightly to meet his hazel gaze.

"You look…" He allows the words to filter into nothing. I've never wanted to impress anyone before. Never craved attention or the validation from anyone in my life. But I want to hear it from him.

"I do?" I quip, my brow arching in question.

"You definitely do." He turns me around,

so we're face to face, and I take in his strong, smooth jawline, his full lips, sharp nose, and those beautiful eyes that shine with everything and nothing all at the same time.

"So do you," I tell him.

"You in that dress…" He shakes his head. "It makes me want to rip it from your body and bend you over in front of this mirror, so I can show you how much I want you." The raw honesty in his words causes a tremble to travel from the top of my head all the way down to my toes.

"If you rip it off, I'll have nothing to wear," I tell him. "And I don't think you want me attending the *dinner* without clothes on." I intend for him to notice the inflection when I mention the word dinner. I'm not sure what they're hiding, but somehow, I know Ares won't give me the full story, even if I ask.

"That's true. I'm the only person allowed to see you naked."

"Right. So, will you tell me what tonight is about?"

"No." Short, clipped, nothing more. "But

you look breathtaking." Ares presses a kiss on my mouth, the minty taste of him has me craving more. "I wish we could run away, never come back to Tynewood."

"Why? It's your home."

When those hazel eyes meet mine, he nods. "It is. But sometimes there's more to life than a house you grew up in. Sometimes the truth clears your ideals and makes you want more."

"Do you enjoy speaking in riddles?"

His mouth tilts into a handsome grin, which makes his eyes sparkle, and I'm once again enamored by Ares Lancaster. He's an asshole at the best of times, but every now and then, he offers a glimpse into the man underneath the cold veneer.

"I like to see you smile." And there it is, the gentleman hiding in the shadows of a normally cold-hearted bastard. "Tonight won't be easy," he informs me.

"What do you mean?"

"You're going to learn more about my father and me, and you'll learn about your dad," he utters with pained contempt. Guilt flashes in his eyes when he sees me wince at the mention of my father. *Does he truly understand the heartache I feel?* Yes. He lost his mother, but it wasn't because of her job or because she was sick.

"How can the past have so much influence on the future?" I turn away from him, not wanting to see the emotions in his gaze anymore. Lowering my head, I stare at my feet. The sparkling heels I'm wearing shimmer with promise, but I know we're about to walk into nothing but war.

"It doesn't have to."

I don't turn to him when he says this because I know the moment I do, I'll reconsider his offer to run away. As much as Ares annoys me at the best of times, he also makes me feel things. He knows deep down I have darkness in me, and it matches his own.

"Look at me, little flower," he insists, but this time, I don't obey. I can't.

Before any more words tumble between us, his hand lands on my back, forcing me to bend for him. The hem of my dress is flicked over my hips, and my panties are bare to him.

"What are you doing?" My question is mumbled. But Ares ignores me as he kicks my legs open. He doesn't wait for me to stop him. His fingers tug the material to the side before slipping inside me as he taunts me.

"You look so fucking good bent over for me," he praises, low and feral as he adds a second finger, opening me, spreading me for him. "Your little pussy is soaked, Dahlia," he tells me something I already know because every pump of his fingers causes my walls to tighten around his ministrations.

"Please, fuck, I need to come," I plead with him. My palms are flat against the mirror, my cheeks are flushed, my eyes wide and shiny with desire, and the way Ares stares at me in the glass makes my knees buckle from the pleasure that's slowly consuming me.

"You're mine," he tells me earnestly, our gazes locked in a heated standoff. I want to refute him, tell him that he's dreaming, but it's not a lie. "Tell me, Dahlia." His request is gravel over my skin, causing a shiver to race down my spine and a shiver to attack my body.

"I'm yours."

"I can't hear you," he taunts as his thumb circles my clit. The motion has fireworks bursting inside me, my vision blurry from an impending orgasm.

"I'm yours, Ares."

"Again," he commands, his fingers fucking me violently, my core dripping with need, with arousal coating his fingers as he toys with me like a rag doll, and my toes curl when he drops down behind me and laps at my body like a starving man.

"I'm yours." My words are whimpered, mewled like a cat in heat because that's what I feel like when Ares' tongue slashes across my body again and again.

"Come on my tongue," he grunts, and my body spasms wildly when he crooks his fingers against the soft part inside me, which has fire bursting through me like an erupting volcano. "That's a good girl," Ares coos. His words wash over me, my mind is lost in the need for release. My body trembling, and at his mercy, just where he likes me. My pussy tightens, pulsing, feeling him stretch me open as he claims me. I've never felt pleasure like this, never had every nerve in my body alive with electric need.

I'm lost in euphoria, in the swirl of desire that's catapulted me from this bedroom into a black hole where all I can do is relent and submit to the man who's played me from day one.

As we descend the stairs, I notice Tarian and Etienne, and between the boys is my best friend. She's dressed in a luxurious silk gown that hugs her curves like a second skin. The bright pink color pops amongst the dark suits in the room, and the moment her gaze lands on me, her eyes light up with excitement.

We rush toward each other, pulling each other in for a hug, and I breathe easy knowing she's okay. I'm still a little wobbly from my orgasm, but Ares' arm snakes around my waist, and he pulls me closer to him.

"Is he here yet?" Ares asks this of Etienne who shakes his head.

The older man who I met briefly, an old friend of Abner, stalks up to us. "You ready for this, Ares?" He questions, his gaze darting between me and the man who's just made my body tingle, in every way possible.

"I told you, he has to agree to this, or I walk." The tension that surrounds us is palpable until a beautiful, tall blonde woman walks up to us, slipping her arm around Tarian's shoulders.

"What's with all the serious faces? It's a party," she guffaws loudly as she pulls the younger man into her chest, which seems to be heaving out of her champagne colored designer dress.

"Mom," Etienne hisses under his breath as he pulls away from her. "Can you please have something to eat, you need to soak up the alcohol," he informs her.

"Oh, my son, ever the levelheaded one."

She chuckles, running a nail over Tarian's shoulder. The bright red of her manicure and the dark material of his jacket is a stark contrast. It's also a reminder that I don't belong in this world. I'm an outsider to the wealth, to the secret society, and to the people who are born into it.

"Excuse us." Ares laces his fingers with mine and practically drags me from the crowd. We make our way through the living room and out onto a patio, which overlooks a dimly lit garden. The land spreads far and wide, dipping into darkness the further away you get from the house.

"Where are we going?"

We come to a stop on the grass. My heels slowly sink into the soft ground, but when Ares spins me around, I take in the monstrosity before us. Three floors of opulent beauty greet me. The windows light up, offering a view of the chandeliers inside. It's breathtaking. I've never seen something as stunning with two turrets, black metal balconies, and the smooth walls of stone. Not even the Lancaster mansion is built to such perfection.

"You drugged me, brought me to a palace, and you're about to serve me up on a platter to your dad?" I question, not looking at Ares. I don't want to see the truth in his eyes, not because I'm scared of coming face to face with Abner, but because I'm afraid of losing Ares.

"Dahlia." Ares turns to me, his gaze locking on mine. "There's something you need to know. Something I haven't told you yet." Every single word he utters makes my body turn rigid. I'm not sure what I'm expecting him to say, but when he opens his mouth again, he tells me something I that tips my world on its axis. "Your father's alive."

TWENTY-NINE

Ares

"WHAT?" HER EYES ARE WIDE WITH SHOCK. "What do you mean?"

I didn't want to do this now. But there's not going to be time when my father arrives. And he'll probably just tell her the truth to hurt her. To see her in agony.

"He's being held in the dungeon where the Sovereign meet. I'm not sure of the details. Tarian is trying to find out more."

When Dahlia blinks, a tear slowly rolls down her cheek, the black mascara that surrounds her pretty eyes looks even darker now that her emotions have escaped. Tracks make strange patterns down her face, and I want to wipe them away. I need to stop the pain that's so clearly etched on her face, but I can't.

I enjoy knowing I'm the one who holds her happiness in my hand. And at the utterance of a word, she's at my mercy. *Where she should be for the rest of her life.* The thought appears and disappears quickly, and I have to breathe deeply to calm my hard on and my heartbeat.

"We'll find him, I'll make this right."

"You mean you'll kill him for murdering your mother," she bites out, taking a step away from me. The truth is, if I didn't know what my father had done, I might have wanted my revenge on Patrick, but it isn't his fault. He was merely a pawn in my father's fucked up games.

"My father threatened yours, the only person who should be paying for any crime is Abner Lancaster."

Her dark brows shoot up at my response. I know she wasn't expecting me to say something like that, to turn on my father, but she doesn't know what I'm capable of. Once I'm hurt, lied to, or even fucked over by someone I trusted, there's no earning back my respect.

"So…" Her voice cracks and I want to pull her into my arms, to revel in her pain and bask in her tears, but I allow her to come to terms with what I just told her. "I mean, he's alive?" Hope springs up in her eyes, the blue bright, shimmering with the tears that sit on her lashes.

Fuck, she's beautiful.

"He is," I confirm. "I don't know if he's been hurt. Knowing my dad, there's a possibility, Patrick won't be the same man you remember." I don't want her to have false hope. Her dad may be hurt beyond recognition, he may even be hanging on by a thread, but if I can give her a proper goodbye, then I will.

"I never understood why Fergus wouldn't allow an open casket," she mutters randomly, which sets the hair on the back of my neck to stand up.

"What did you say?"

She crosses her arms as if she's trying to hold herself together. "I asked for a final goodbye at my dad's funeral. Fergus was the

323

one who said it would be best not to open it, he told me I should remember my dad as he was when he was alive."

As if puzzle pieces fall into place in the frayed image in my mind, I finally understand why my father wanted me to look into Fergus. He didn't want suspicion on their connection. Pulling my phone from my pocket, I hit dial on Tarian's number.

"What are you doing?" Dahlia questions.

I'm suddenly freezing, but it has nothing to do with the weather. I'm finally seeing more of my father than I ever wanted to. I'm learning about the man I always looked up to and realizing he's nothing more than a monster. Three rings and Tarian's on the other end of the line.

"Yo, man," he says. "What's up?"

"I need everything you can find on Fergus, the partner," I tell him while staring at Dahlia who's blinking back tears.

"Yeah, I can look into it. I only did a narrow search a few weeks ago," he tells me. "What happened?"

"I have a feeling the asshole is working for my dad. I just don't know why or when it happened."

"Do you think this Fergus dude is part of the Sovereign?" The million-dollar question that I should know the answer to. I should know every name in Father's contact lists, but Abner made sure we were all blind to what he was doing. Maybe, just maybe, the Crowns will fall, and it will be the new regime that takes them out.

"I don't know, but if he is, he's going to need a fucking army to fight me on this. I want to know every dirty detail he has hiding in those closets, and we need it tonight, before dinner."

We have thirty minutes before guests start arriving, but I have faith in my best friend. He's good, he's the best, and I know he's the only one who can find out what we need.

"You know you can count on me. I'll be in Billy's office working on this," Tarian tells me, and I can hear the smile in this voice.

"Okay, thanks." I hang up and turn to

Dahlia.

Her big blue eyes lock on mine. "Tell me, Ares," she pleads, nearing me. "Tell me, I'll see him again." I want to say no, I want to tell her that she might not be so lucky to find him alive, but I can't bring myself to do it.

So, instead of offering her a brutal truth, I nod. "You will. Somehow, I'll make sure you get to see him again."

I know what the pain of losing a parent brings. There are so many things I would love to tell my mother right now. But I can't. So I give Dahlia some form of hope.

I pull her into my arms, allowing her to nuzzle into my chest. Her perfume fills my senses, and I wonder how I'm going to let her go when the time comes.

"We need to head back inside," I tell her.

Dahlia steps away from me, tilting her head back and smiles up at me. "Thank you for giving me this. I know it's not—"

"Just leave it be." My words are cold, more aloof than I want, but emotion will only stir up shit right now. "Let's go."

I drag her along behind me, and I pray for the first time in my life that things will go our way. That one of us won't be killed.

We're all seated at the table when the door opens with a whoosh. The tension that fills the room chokes the air that fills my lungs.

"So, this is where you've been hiding?" My father utters when he reaches the table. His tall, formidable figure looms over me as his hand squeezes on my shoulder. When I was younger, I would cower. I'd be shaking because I wanted to impress him, but not anymore. I'm more of a man than he will ever be.

The chair scrapes along the tiles as I shove it back, the sound bouncing off the walls as I stand to meet his gaze dead on. My spine straight, shoulders squared.

"I don't hide."

"Oh?" He tips his head to the side as he regards me. Every person in the room has stopped moving. It's as if everyone is holding their breath to see the showdown between father and son.

"It's time the Sovereign moves into the twenty-first century," I tell him. "You're no longer in charge. Philipe is the head chair, and if he allows a vote, the four of us will all be in favor." My confidence doesn't waver, and I want to pull Dahlia into my arms to show him I'm in charge.

"Really? You think your brother is going to go against me?" A dark chuckle escapes my father's mouth, and his eyes shimmer with a challenge. There's violence swirling in the air, and his hands land on either of my shoulders. "You want that little brat?" He bites out, glaring at my girl behind me.

"She's already mine." I'm not backing down. I've made the decision, and he can never stop me. I know he's shocked at my show of confidence.

"Have you forgotten what her father did to your mother?"

"No, but then again, what is it you *had* her

father do?" I counter, challenging him. I doubt he'll admit the truth with people listening. Etienne's mother is here, and as much as I know she hates the society, she's never hated someone as much as she has my father. She wouldn't think twice about calling the cops if she knew the truth.

Abner glares at me, then slowly nods. "Then you'll play for it."

"What?"

He shrugs as if he's talking about the weather. "We play for it. You know the Sovereign doesn't allow you to just get what you want without a challenge."

"Fine. What do you want me to do?" I shrug him off me, stepping back and folding my arms in front of my chest. My father and I are the same height, so nothing he does intimidates me.

"Hide and seek," he tells me. "She'll have a minute head start, and we'll go after her." He waves his hand in the air, gesturing to the darkness outside the window. The depth of the forest in this cold weather could kill someone if they got lost, especially since Dahlia's wearing a goddamned silk dress.

"No."

"No? If you want this, that's my only offer." He glances at the beauty behind me. "Take off your shoes. And go." He lifts his watch, tapping the timer. "You have one minute to get as far as possible." Abner reaches into his jacket and pulls out his knife. A large hunting knife I didn't expect him to be wearing to a dinner party. But then again, he's in the home of an enemy.

"What?" Dahlia's hiss comes from behind me.

"You're running out of time," he warns her as he steps back, twisting the sleek silver in his hand. "Don't let me find you, I like to slice pretty girls." The honest confession turns my stomach.

The shuffle of material from behind me has me spinning on my heel. Dahlia's shoes lay on the ground beside her. She leans up on her tiptoes and presses a soft kiss to my cheek. And then, she's out the door.

I turn back to my father, a man who is now a stranger. "This is fucked up." My voice is a low, angry growl, but I know I'll beat him at his game.

"You wanted to step up to the table, son. The Sovereign enjoy challenges, and they enjoy Crowns who can hold their own. Can you?" He steps around me and makes his way to the door, and like the sheep he thinks we are, we follow the wolf as he goes on the hunt for his prey.

What he doesn't know is… he'll be the one begging for mercy.

THIRTY

Ares

It's been ten minutes, and we still haven't found her. Tarian, Etienne, and I have been walking through the darkness as we follow behind my father. He's excited by this bullshit, which only confirms my decision.

Tension tightens my muscles, and I'm close to snapping. My throat is dry from calling her name, but it seems my little flower is well versed in hiding.

My father glares at me, rage filling his expression. He's given me a choice, and I made my decision. There's so much darkness inside him, so much evil, I don't know how I never saw it before.

All my life I wanted to be like him, I wanted him to approve of me, to be proud of me. And now I'm doing the one thing he would never have thought. I'm going against my family, against his orders, and it infuriates him.

"This will never be over." Abner's warning rings in my ears as he nears me. The man I grew up with, the one person who never gave me the attention I wanted so badly, stands before me with rage in his eyes.

He reminds me of a tyrant ruling over a kingdom who hates him. A group of people who would rather see him dead.

"No, it's not over," I acquiesce. "But she's mine." Determination is evident in my voice, causing him to arch his brow at me in question. "I chose her. Not this." I wave my hand in the air between us. "This society you think will hide your fucked-up indiscretions is no longer yours."

Before we take another step, I hear a branch cracking in the distance and head toward it, before my father can even second guess where he's going. I feel him hot on my heels when I come to find Dahlia on her knees.

He ignores my jibe and chuckles. "If you don't kill her now, I will hunt you forever. And you know that I'll never stop until your life is a misery." I don't doubt him at all. I think he'll enjoy it. This cat and mouse game will be his greatest victory.

I turn my gaze toward Dahlia. Her dress is caked in mud, but she's never looked more beautiful. Tears stream down her cheeks, making the black streaks of her make up stain her pretty face. This is what I wanted for so long, but it's no longer what my focus is. She's right here, and all I want to do is save her from the fucker who wants her dead.

"Ares," Abner's voice is a deep, rage-filled growl, "kill her now, or I'll make sure you both end up six-feet under." He shoves the knife into my hand, and my thumb swipes over the wooden handle, feeling the crest of the Sovereign on the weapon.

"Do it," she bites out. "Just fucking do it, Ares. End it." Her voice is tainted with anguish, dripping in disdain for the man who's cruelly looming over her.

How can she ask me to do this?

She used to hate me just as much as I hated her.

But now... I love her.

Emotion is dangerous.

It produces a war within oneself, so cruel and completely volatile, and nothing can stop it.

The good and bad that everyone claims to be is nothing more than feelings toying with us. Ruling us. Whether it's love or hate, anger or happiness, we're nothing but pawns to it.

"I'm the one in charge." Abner stalks closer to her, and my grip tightens around the handle of the knife.

"You're nothing more than a coward," Dahlia bites out, tugging on the skirts of her dress. The white material that was once pure is stained with the sins of the past and the lies of the present.

"Ares," my best friend's voice startles me from the stupor I'm caught in. He hands me his iPhone, which is open on an email he'd hacked. The truth glares at me, clear and true.

Cutting my gaze to my father first then at Dahlia, I head toward the woman who's both enamored me and stolen my fucking heart and soul and take a step closer to her. My hand shoots out, gripping her long dark hair as I tug her by the strands, ensuring she doesn't look away.

I lean in, crouching down, so we're eye to eye. Her mouth curls in a satisfied smirk, matching my own emotion-fueled glare. It's time to end this. End everything. No more games. No more bullshit. I want to tell her to leave me, I should give her an out. But I can't.

"Come with me," I tell her in a hushed whisper.

"What?" She gasps when I tug harder, causing her to whimper.

"Ares, I'm not waiting a minute longer. End the Milton girl, or I'll do it. And when I do, you'll watch her bleed out all over that pretty white dress."

"If you don't come with me, you'll be dead by morning." The promise is in my eyes, I know she can see it because her own pretty glare widens. Those blue orbs that hold me, hostage, now tell me of the fear that's so clear in her expression.

"Why are you choosing me?" Her question is warranted. I made her life hell, and yet, here I am, making sure she survives this.

"Because I didn't expect to fall in love," I respond.

Dahlia's soft, surprised intake of breath is evidence that she wasn't expecting it, neither was I. Releasing Dahlia, I offer her my hand, praying with all I have she'll take it.

When she accepts it, I pull her to her feet. Her beautiful dress is filthy, but I tug her along behind me. We head up the garden, back to the house. I know this can go either way, so I keep Dahlia in front of me, and my father behind. If he tries anything, it will be me he kills.

"I won't let you walk out of here." Abner's voice is loud and clear, and the click and cock of a gun has me stalling all movement. We're stopped in the living room with Billy, Mrs. Durand, and Philipe, standing there watching us.

I wonder what the hell my brother was thinking supporting a man like this. Shaking my head, I can't help but grin at the stupid lies I've believed all these years.

Granted, he's our father, our family, but I can't justify his evil deeds anymore. He's fucked with too many lives, and it's time that comes to an end. I turn my body fully toward him, pushing Dahlia behind me. I don't want her hurt.

"Do it." He glares at me for a long while, too long. He raises the 9mm toward me, aiming directly for my heart. The place where I used to have hate is no longer beating with revenge, it's thudding with emotion that's so foreign to me—love. And it's due to the woman who made me feel.

"You're willing to die for her?"

"Take the shot and see," I challenge. I no longer have fear ruling me. I don't even feel as if this is real. Perhaps, I'm dreaming, and my father isn't holding a gun at me. "I'm your son, I'll never be anything else. But remember this, once you pull that trigger, the Sovereign falls apart. You're no longer head of the table."

I shouldn't poke the sleeping bear.

I shouldn't challenge the man who holds my life in his hands.

"Ares, what are you doing?" Dahlia's sweet, earnest whisper filters into my ear and I can't help but smile. As much as we fight, I know she cares.

"Tonight, the Sovereign will lose a new member." My father's voice bounces from the walls as Billy walks out, his face impassive, but his eyes hold the *I told you, so* I was expecting. I knew the danger, and I'm prepared.

A shot rings out. A blur of people, bodies moving, and then I'm crumpling to my knees. The next few seconds spill free so quickly that I don't register the pain until I'm on the floor. Until I feel Dahlia's hands on mine, her voice screaming loudly.

There's movement all around me. But the searing agony that's burning through my chest is unbearable. Dahlia's worried gaze, then Tarian's pair of blue eyes, along with the dark brown of Etienne's all appear before me.

"I..." My throat is dry, painful. I want to say something, but they're telling me to be quiet. Dahlia presses something on my chest, heavily putting all her weight on it, which isn't much.

My mind is blank.

My eyelids feel heavy, and as much as I try to fight the sleepiness, I can't.

And soon, everything is black.

THIRTY-ONE
Dahlia

THE NEXT FEW SECONDS PASS BY IN A BLUR. Tears stream from my face, mud cakes every inch of my dress, and there's blood all over my hands. I'm dragged from Ares' body by a stronghold on my arms. And even as I scream and attempt to fight off the strength of the stranger, I know, I won't be able to.

My glare pins Abner to the spot, but all he can do is smirk. The asshole shot his own son, and he's smiling. Evil burns in his eyes, and I realize there's no more hope left. I'm almost certain he killed my father.

"You are mine," he sneers, meeting my gaze, ignoring the tears rolling over my cheeks. The man who's holding me back isn't someone I know or someone I've ever seen before. There's a reason he's here: to aide Abner Lancaster in destroying everything I hold dear.

The voices come to me in a whir, everything's blurry, and even though I try to focus, I can't.

"We have to get him to the hospital."

"There's a slow heartbeat."

"We don't know if he's going to make it."

"I don't think he's breathing."

My heart thuds as it attacks my ribcage like it's fighting its way out of my chest.

"Abner, you're not leaving here with her." This comes from Billy, the man who owns the house. There's a standoff between them, as I watch Tarian and Etienne take Ares away. He's barely moving, and the agony that lances my chest is so acute, I struggle to pull in air.

My lungs don't work. They're fighting against what I already know. The bullet is in his chest; it's lodged in his heart, I'm sure of it. And somehow, I feel the pain in my own heart as well.

The smell of blood fills the room. Tariana

and Etienne move swiftly around me, but nobody's shocked at the events of tonight. I suppose all the guests know about the Sovereign. They all know about the evil secret society that my father was a part of.

"You can't tell me what I will or won't do. When you stepped down, you made your choice," Abner tells Billy in a low, gravelly tone that instills fear in me right to my core. Then, those familiar eyes are on me again. "Take her to the car," he informs the man holding me.

"No! I want to see Ares!" My voice is a high-pitched squeal. "Let me go!"

My voice cracks when I'm dragged out of the living room with eyes pinned on me from everyone standing around as if this is normal. This isn't a normal fucking life. None of this is okay. How can everyone just stand by and watch? My body is slung into the backseat of a blacked-out SUV, and the moment I'm left alone, my attempt at opening the door is thwarted by the lock clicking in place.

I watch in horror as Etienne's car speeds down the drive, and I'm left alone. There's nothing I can do from the backseat of the car, I'm locked in. I don't have my phone or my purse.

My vision is blurry, and I can't stop sobbing when I'm joined by Abner and the bodyguard who locked me in, in the first place.

"Please, let me see Ares?" I plead, hoping that there's a shred of humanity in the man who's sitting in the passenger seat.

He flips the visor down, glancing at me in the mirror. "Do you really think my son would choose you over something he's wanted his whole life?"

Rage surges inside me, my blood burns in agony, and my frayed nerves are at the end of their tether. "He already has," I bite out. "Don't you see it? He chose me in there."

"He wasn't thinking clearly. I'll make sure that when he wakes up, he'll have his priorities straight." Abner's voice is cold, filled with power and violence. "Tell me, Dahlia," he says, "if I made you choose between your father and Ares. Who would be the man you'd choose to save?"

My heart catapults into my throat, and I can't swallow past the lump of emotion that's threatening to choke me. More tears spill free from my eyes when we pull up to the Lancaster house.

"Where is he? Where's my dad?" Inching closer to the front seat, I grip the headrest in an attempt to stop myself from clawing at the bastard's face. I want to make him pay. I want to punish him just as much as he's done to everyone around him.

The car comes to a stop in a garage that doesn't provide much light, and I wonder if we're under part of the house. The space has an eerie feeling, which causes my stomach to churn with anxiety and fear.

"Your father is a guest of mine," Abner tells me, before shoving open the door and exiting the vehicle. Moments later, I'm dragged from the seat, and a piece of silver masking tape is slapped over my mouth. My hands are bound behind me, and I'm being lifted over the shoulder of the bodyguard whose name I still don't know.

My breaths come in short spurts. I'm trembling from head to toe, praying for Ares to live, praying for my father to be alive, and begging that I'll make it out of this with the men I care for, the men I love.

I'm deposited on a couch that overlooks the garden. There's nowhere to run, no way to get off the property without the security team finding out. A young man stalks into the living room, his eyes are the deepest green I've ever seen. His hair is dark, like Ares', and his expression is filled with thunder.

"Kidnapping?" He questions Abner. "This wasn't part of our agreement."

"Don't talk to me as if I'm your soldier, boy," Abner bites out, gripping the younger man by the shirt and hoisting him up as if he weighs nothing.

Philipe Lancaster.

Ares' older brother.

"Take her down to the dungeon, she wants to see her daddy dearest. She has one hour. I'm heading to the hospital to bring Ares home."

A phone rings shrilly from somewhere in

the house, but it doesn't sound for very long, and I wonder if they have a maid or butler who answers calls.

"Sure, I can look after the princess," Philipe mutters. Disdain paints his handsome face. He pulls me to my feet by my muddied dress and practically drags me behind him.

"Oh, and Dahlia..." Abner says, "make sure you say your goodbyes, your father will be dead by morning." The older man saunters out of the room and disappears from sight before I'm stumbling behind Philipe again. We reach a locked door, which looks like it's made of steel. Just behind us is the kitchen.

Steps lead us down into darkness, but it doesn't last long, because Philipe snaps a switch on the wall, and soon enough, we're bathed in the yellow glow of a lamp that hangs from the center of a low ceiling.

"One hour." His voice reminds me far too much of Ares, and my heart aches for the boy, the man who I've fallen for. The tape is ripped from my mouth, causing me to wince and whimper in agony.

He leaves my hands bound, but he unlocks the gate and shoves me into the cell that stinks of sweat, blood, and urine. And then I'm alone with a hunched-up body, which doesn't move from the corner of the small square prison.

"Dad?"

THIRTY-TWO
Dahlia

THE SOUND OF SHUFFLING COMES FROM THE huddle in the corner. I watch him move, and the moment those familiar blue eyes meet mine, I fall to my knees.

"Daddy?"

"Dahli?" He croaks, moving toward me. The moment the dim light hits his face, I cringe, noticing the scars that mar his once handsome face. "Why are you here?"

"I-I... Abner... he brought me here," I tell him as tears stream down my cheeks, burning with emotion as they drip from my chin, soaking the material of my dress.

"I never wanted you here," Dad tells me. "You don't belong in this town. It's filled with darkness." My father doesn't make a move to touch me or to come closer than he already is. His clothes are dirty, caked in filth that's become part of the material.

"I don't understand why you never told me about this. Why did you let Fergus tell me you're dead?"

"That wasn't me. Abner orchestrated everything that you heard about my disappearance. Fergus was meant to step up as one of the Crowns, but he didn't agree with the way Abner ran things. However," my dad whispers, the tone of his voice is low, scratchy, and I wonder when he's last had a drink of water or something warm to eat. "He still did odd jobs for the man. I didn't know."

"So all these years he's been working with Mr. Lancaster?"

Dad nods, shifting on his heels, as he crouches down, curling himself into a ball. He groans, low and feral. When he looks up at me again, I see the agony in his eyes.

"I wish they'd just kill me and let it be over with."

"Don't say that," I cry as the memory of

his funeral flashes in my mind as if it were yesterday. I cried, I bawled my eyes out, kneeling on the soft, wet earth beside the hole I thought my father's body was being lowered into.

"Dahli, my sweet girl," Dad murmurs, "I've lived my life, I've done things I'm not proud of, and most of the things I did were to keep you safe. Protected. I failed in so many ways."

"You never failed me." Confidence burns through me, and I can no longer take it, shuffling toward him, I pull my dad into a hug. "Tell me," I start, nervous about taking the leap, but I know I have to. "Did you kill Ares' mother?" Guilt swims in his pain-filled eyes, and I have my answer without him even uttering a word.

He nods slowly. "I did. I shot her in the foyer of their home." My father's voice is raspy when he admits it. "Abner told me if I didn't do it, he'd come for you. He wanted to kill you. He stole your mother, and he would've taken you, too."

"He stole mom?"

"She loved him for a long time." His admission makes my chest hurt. "I couldn't save her, but I could save you." Dad pulls me into a hold, keeping me warm in the chilliness of the cell. And I wonder if I'll ever see my mother again because I have a feeling she's probably still alive.

A clank sounds behind me, and moments later, footsteps echo around us, reminding me that we're in a cell, in the dungeon of a mansion in the middle of a sleepy town that's run by evil.

"It's because of you, my brother is fighting for his life," Philipe tells me.

Releasing my father, I spin on my heel and pin him with a glare. "Because of me? Why don't you go up there and ask your father who pulled the goddamned trigger?"

"This," Philipe hisses through clenched teeth as he pulls his sleeve up, and I take note of the ink on his skin. The emblem that Ares has tattooed on his back is clear as day on Philipe's forearm. "This is what it's all about.

A brotherhood."

"And your *brotherhood* thinks it's okay to kill innocent people? Even if it's your own flesh and blood?" The fire that burns through me comes across in my words. I want him to see how wrong this is. If I can get through to him, maybe, just maybe, he'll let me and my dad go.

"No," Philipe nods. "It's not right to kill innocent people, but—"

"But your father shot your brother," I interrupt him. My fingers curl around the bars of the cell, and I tug and pull at the gate, as frustration flows through me like a river of lava.

Philipe's green eyes shimmer with annoyance, but he makes no attempt to get closer to me or open the gate. As if we're two chess pieces on a board, I wait for him to make his move. I've said all I can, there's nothing that will change his mind after my little tirade.

"I can see why my brother is so enamored with you," he finally tells me.

"He did what?" My father's crackling

voice breaks through our conversation. "No, you're not to associate with any of these boys. None of the Sovereign can keep you safe."

"Ares is the reason I'm still alive," I tell my dad. "I love him."

"What?" Both Philipe and my dad utter the one-word question in shock. Flitting my gaze between the two astonished men, I nod.

"I am. I love Ares. He understands me, he knows me," I tell them, but the pain in my chest reminds me that he's still in the hospital, and I have no idea if he's still alive. If he's survived the gunshot, the surgery, I wonder what will become of us.

Maybe I'm being a stupid girl.

Would he ever walk away from the Sovereign for me?

"My brother may have done stupid things in the past," Philipe tells me as he unlocks the cell, waiting for me to exit. Once I'm beside him, he shuts the door and slides the lock into place. "But I think this time, he's fucked up royally. My father will never allow you to sit at the table."

"She's a woman," my father bites out. "She cannot be Crowned," he continues, and his words slice me open, flaying me with the anger-filled command, "I won't allow it."

"It's not up to you," I tell him. "If I want to be at that table, if I want to wear the mark of the Sovereign, I'll do it. One way or another." I keep my voice low, it's a promise, a vow. I've made up my mind, and nobody, not some old custom, will stop me from being beside Ares as he rules the brotherhood with Etienne, Tarian, and Philipe.

"Your daughter is very strong," Philipe remarks from beside me, his gaze locked on my father's. "She'll probably take us all down. She will become a Crown." A chuckle rumbles in his throat, the sound is almost comforting because it reminds me of *him*, of Ares.

"Over my dead body," Dad mutters. "Dahlia, think about this," he pleads. "This isn't the life I wanted for you. That's why I left Tynewood."

"You may not have wanted this life for me, Dad, but I'm in it." Stepping closer to the cell, I watch him hobble toward me. He looks nothing like the man I grew up with. The long dark beard covers half his face, the black marks of soot and dirt cover what I recall was his once perfect, angular cheekbones. And his eyes have lost their happiness. "I can't run from something. I'm not you."

He stares at me for a long while before he acquiesces. "You're a good girl." The words fall from his lips, but before the last word has calmed my heartbeat, my dad's hands shoot through the bars, gripping my neck and pulling me closer, causing my breath to stifle.

"Dad—"

"You will die before you become a Crown." The dark edge to his voice scares me, and his grip tightens until I see stars behind my eyelids. I'm fighting for breath in one second, and in the next, a gunshot rings through the air. The bullet sends my father tumbling backward, falling in a slump on the floor.

A scream ricochets through my chest and bounces off the walls. Arms envelop me as more tears stain my cheeks as they trickle in heated rivulets across my face. Philipe's warm breath is at my ear.

"Calm the fuck down," he bites out when I kick at him. "If you don't, I'll tie you up again," he warns, and I stall all movement. The pain that stings my neck is agonizing, and I'm speechless when I realize my father tried to kill me.

He wanted me dead.

He never wanted me to be a Crown.

But not everyone gets what they want.

Until now.

"Take me to see Ares, please? I need to know more about the Sovereign. I want to learn about my heritage that's linked to the society."

Respect paints Philipe's handsome face, and he nods, offering me a hand before leading me to my future.

THIRTY-THREE

Ares

"HE WAS."

"But I don't understand why he would do that."

"He loves her."

"Does she love him?"

My eyes crack open, the glare of white hospital lights greets me. At the end of the bed, near the metal foot end, is my father and brother. They're arguing about something, but I can't quite make out what it is.

I watch them for a moment, taking note of the two men in my life who were meant to be role models and turned out... differently. My hands and feet feel as if I've had them in ice. I'm cold even though I'm covered with a blanket and a sheet.

"Hey," I greet my brother, making sure my focus is on him, not the man who shot me. "Where's Dahlia?"

"She's outside," Philipe tells me.

"Son," Dad says, but I can't deal with him right now. He shot me, and this time, he will pay. I'll make sure of it.

"Call Tarian in here," I tell my brother, and he nods. There's a solemnness to him, and when his forest colored eyes meet mine, I notice the guilt sitting in his stare. He knows what happened. Would Dahlia have gotten through to him? Has she made him see that what our father did was wrong?

"Ares," Dad says, causing me to turn to him as soon as Philipe is out the door. "I was trying to look out for you. That girl is dangerous. She's a liability that we don't need."

"No, Dad. She's a liability that *you* don't need. I love her, and I'm not going to walk away from her because you deemed the relationship unacceptable. You shot me. Do you even realize you could've killed me?"

359

Tarian enters the room before my father can say a word. He glances between us, and I can see he's unsure as to what's happening. I shouldn't even be talking to the asshole who shot me, but I have a plan.

"Tar," I greet him with an easy smile. The moment I shift to sit up, pain shoots through me, and I can't help but groan. This is ridiculous. I can't do shit. "I need that information you got for me," I tell him.

He offers a small nod before handing me my phone. While I scroll through my phone, I have to bite the inside of my cheek to keep from grinning. My best friend came through. I look over at my father. "You're not getting away with all your bullshit anymore, Dad," I tell him, hoping he doesn't see what I'm doing. "Having Patrick Milton kill mom was one thing, trying to shoot your own son because he chose to live his life, that's another. What else have you done?"

Tarian and I turn our attention to my dad who's turning red with rage, but I'm no longer afraid. He can't kill me now; there are witnesses, so he has to take my inquiries and either respond or walk out.

"I did what needed to be done," he informs me, both hands on the mattress beside me. "One day, when you're head of that table, you'll see that what I did was warranted. Killing your mother was one order that Milton actually obeyed. He was a liability."

"It seems everyone who doesn't agree with you is a liability."

"I will rule this family the way I see fit. Dahlia Milton will either walk out of this town without my son, or she'll be buried on our property, and you can visit her when I'm not around."

My blood turns to ice at his words. I shake my head. "No, Dad. Let me tell you what's going to happen, you're going to prison."

A sharp, cruel laugh escapes him at my words. I knew he wouldn't believe me. How could he? I'm his son, and I'm meant to love him. To respect him. But I lost that the moment I realized what a monster he truly is.

The door swishes open, causing me to

glance at the entrance. Dahlia is standing there beside Philipe. She's changed into a pair of gray sweatpants that look awfully familiar. The T-shirt that's hanging from her slim frame is also mine, and I want to smile.

"Get her the fuck out of here," Dad rages like a tyrant.

"I'm not going anywhere," Dahlia tells him. "You kept my father prisoner for three long years, you tortured him, you made sure to break not only his will but his mind. And you expect me to cower because I'm merely a teenager and a woman?" Her voice is filled with the kind of anger and rage I've never seen on her before.

She's fucking exquisite.

My dick agrees when she steps forward with confidence.

Even though I'm in pain, and I can't move without wincing, she still makes my body react, turning me on like nobody else ever has. I always thought I had power over her, but it's her who reigns her power over me.

Dad rounds the end of the bed, stalking

toward the woman who has burrowed her way into my heart and mind. I want to go to her, to stand between her and the old man, but Philipe shakes his head at me.

He's got this.

He's on our side.

"Listen to me, little girl," Abner Lancaster declares, but he doesn't know his hold on us is about to be broken. He's about to go down, and nothing he says can stop it from happening. "I'll see to it that you're in the ground with your poor excuse for a father."

I expect my girl to do something, to slap him, but she only smiles. "You know who a poor excuse for a father is?" She doesn't wait for him to respond when she continues, "You are. Buying your sons' love with a seat at an old table that sits in the goddamned basement of a church, doesn't make you right and it sure as hell doesn't make you innocent."

"What are you talking about?"

"You killed people. You had my father mutilated because you can't stand not being in control." Dahlia's normally sweet tone is filled with contempt, and I've never been more turned on than seeing her stand up to my father.

His hand shoots out, but before he can make contact with Dahlia's face, Philipe grips his wrist, their gazes locked on each other— father and son.

"I wouldn't do that if I were you." My brother's words are a warning. He could take our father, he's undoubtedly strong enough.

"Oh? And you're on the little bandwagon to have a *woman* sit at your table?"

"You're going away for a long time, Dad," Philipe says. "All those documents from your office, the ones you kept in the safe, are in the hands of the FBI." The smirk that curls my brother's lips is pure satisfaction. "You'll never see the light of day again. And here's a piece of advice -remember that bending over in prison is a no-no."

The low, gravelly tone of Abner's laugh bounces off the walls of the hospital room as he looks at each of us. "You really think you can take me out?" The door slides open, and

Etienne walks in. He's followed by two men in suits who look like the goddamned Men in Black.

"Mr. Lancaster," one of them says, looking directly at Dad. "We would like a word." The silence that now fills the space is thick, heavy with anticipation. What will daddy dearest do? Will he attempt to lie his way out of this?

"Of course, my sons will call my lawyer."

"No need, sir, we already have one waiting for you. Unfortunately, it doesn't look like he'll be much help."

Dad turns to glare at me. "You won't get away with this," he tells me. He believes his lies. He truly thought I couldn't win this war, but I just did.

THIRTY-FOUR

Dahlia

"Come here," Ares commands from his bed. It took a week for him to finally come home from the hospital. Even though he's adamant he doesn't want to live in the house, we have no choice for now.

My gran has spent more time here looking after him than she has at home. Something tells me she approves of Ares and me. I make my way toward the bed and settle on the mattress next to him.

"I don't know what I ever did to deserve you," he tells me as he pulls me into his arms. A small wince of pain scrunches his face. "You're staying here tonight, I need to get my dick wet."

"Fuck you," I bite out, but he chuckles. "It

seems like you're feeling better."

"I am, and that means I can make you scream my name again and again." A smirk appears on his handsome face, his full lips tilted in such a way that makes small dimples form in his cheeks.

"You're far too confident, Mr. Lancaster," I tell him, attempting to scoot up the bed, so I'm more comfortable in the crook of his arm.

"I have to be, I heard girls like that sort of thing," he teases, pressing his lips to my forehead. The tips of his fingers draw circles on my arm, forcing goosebumps to rise on my exposed flesh.

"What girls are you trying to impress?" I ask, keeping my voice low, and attempting to sound nonchalant. Even though we haven't talked about what's going on between us, I wonder briefly if we're just friends with benefits, or if there's something more happening.

"Well, since you asked," Ares starts, "there's this one girl, she's rather young, but I like that she's a spitfire." The gravel in his voice makes my thighs squeeze together.

"Oh? I thought you preferred your girls to drop to their knees for you?" Our banter is light and playful, but when I glance up and meet those hazel eyes, I see it shining back at me—love.

"I definitely do, so if you're offering, I'll take you up on it." He winks playfully, earning him a swat on the stomach. "Ouch, you have to kiss it better now," he tells me earnestly, and an idea comes to mind.

I pull away, scooting to my knees, I tug his T-shirt up to his chest, exposing his toned stomach to my gaze. His muscles tense and release as I lean in and blow soft breaths on his smooth skin.

"What are you doing?"

"I'm obliging," I tell him. Darting my tongue out, I trace the dips of his abs, slowly, teasing him with the warmth of my mouth. "I thought you'd like it."

"Jesus," Ares hisses when I press a kiss to the bulge that's practically bursting from his boxer briefs. Shoving the sheet down, I tug his underwear down and grip the thick shaft that's hard as steel.

Taking him into my mouth, I slowly, teasingly suck while maintaining eye contact with him. As I feel his cock nudge the back of my throat, the power I have over him in this moment is intoxicating

I close my eyes and focus on the feel of the silky flesh in my mouth and take him slightly deeper, breathing through my gag reflex.

"Shit, little flower," Ares hisses once more as he fists his hands in my hair, holding me steady as his hips rise and fall slowly as he takes control. That's one thing about him, relinquishing himself to anyone is unacceptable, but I don't mind and attempt to smile as he grunts in pleasure as he uses my mouth.

My one hand snakes down between my thighs. I'm wet, needy, and I can't help but moan as I circle my clit, which, in turn, causes Ares to groan, lust heavily laced in the sound. We move in sync, my fingers, and his cock, in and out. Pleasure zips through me, my body coming alive at the feel of him throbbing on my tongue.

"I'm going... oh, fuck..." I watch in awe as he finds pleasure and empties himself in my mouth. "Fuck, Dahlia." He moans as he slowly slips from between my lips. I rise up, making a show of swallowing his release, which only makes him groan again. "You're a naughty girl," Ares grins.

"I thought you liked it?"

"Oh, I definitely do," he nods, scooting down, he crooks his finger. "Come here, sit on my face. I want that pussy." A blush burns my cheeks at his words, but it doesn't take him long to tug me toward the pillows. My panties are shoved aside the second I'm kneeling over his handsome face.

Ares darts his tongue out, causing me to whimper. Eliciting sounds from deep in my gut, the man I love licks and laves at me, his tongue dipping into me as his fingers taunt and tease my clit. My thighs are shaking, my grip on the headboard is white-knuckle tight.

"Ares, oh, oh, please." A plea falls from

my lips as I roll my hips, using his tongue to generate the pressure I need. He responds by pumping two fingers into me. In and out. Faster and faster.

My body locks as pure, animalistic pleasure rockets from my head to my toes. And seconds later, I'm chanting his name as I soak his tongue with my orgasm. My knees are wobbling as I cry out another pleasured moan when Ares teases my back entrance.

"No, not yet," I manage to mumble, causing him to chuckle beneath me. It takes me a few moments to move beside him, taking in his mouth that's still shining with my juices.

"Soon, I'll own all of you, little flower," Ares tells me confidently while licking his lips. "So fucking sweet." He pulls me in, pressing a kiss to my lips, and I can taste myself on him. "Dahlia," he starts, "I love you."

Three words.

My mouth falls open in shock. I never expected him to say it. Even though we've been through hell, which has brought us closer together and solidified our relationship,

I never thought for one second that Ares could love.

His eyes shimmer as he regards me, and I can see he's holding his breath. He's waiting for my answer. "I love you, too." It's true, I do love him. We're both still young, but I have a feeling that whatever happens between Ares Lancaster and me, he'll always be in my life.

I stare at the tombstone that has my father's name engraved on it. At the top of the hill, beside the church where the Sovereign meet, my father lies in a grave six feet under. When I watched him die, I knew I had to do something with my life. I didn't want what happened to him to steer me in the wrong direction.

At nineteen, I should be out partying, but instead, I'm about to be crowned by a secret society. I'm about to become one of the Gilded Sovereign. I'm changing history and the future, and all I want is for him to be proud of me.

With all the evidence Tarian and Philipe found, Abner Lancaster was arrested. He had deep pockets, that's for sure. From what I understand, they had to dig deep to find someone who wasn't on the Sovereign payroll. They had to find a man who wouldn't be scared to put the leader of a secret society in jail.

But that doesn't stop what's coming. Abner promised one thing that we would be sorry we double-crossed him, and I have a feeling we won't be living a peaceful existence until we eradicate all the evil from the Sovereign.

"Goodbye, Dad." My voice sounds foreign to me. I don't know how to feel: the sadness has gone, and it's been replaced with indifference. My father hurt me, he wanted me dead, and he would've succeeded if Philipe hadn't stepped in and saved me. I wonder what he would've done had I died. Would he have been sad?

"Are you ready?" Ares' voice comes from behind me, causing me to pivot. He looks so handsome dressed in a suit and tie.

"I am." He takes my hand and leads me to the Maserati, helping me slip into the passenger seat. Tonight, we meet with the older Crowns who have since stepped down. They have each offered their full support once a court date is set for Abner. After watching him shoot his own son, they came to their senses and realized the man they thought was their equal was nothing more than a criminal.

"Are you okay?" Ares places a hand on my thigh as he speeds down the road toward the university. Thankfully, we're not headed to the church. With the gala dinner being held in the large hall at school, everyone from town will be there.

Looking at Ares, I offer a smile. "I will be," I tell him. "I'm just worried about Rukaiya." It seems my best friend and her father disappeared. As soon as the FBI arrested Abner, they had a team go to Rukaiya's house, but it was empty.

"We'll find her," Ares promises with a small smile that makes my heart catapult in my chest. As happy as I feel being with Ares, knowing his father is locked up tight, there's a niggling deep down that Rukaiya, and her dad will be back. And we'll have to deal with them one way or another.

EPILOGUE

Ares

WATCHING HER AT THE TABLE, THE NEEDLE piercing flesh as it skims across the smooth, creamy skin that I've only just licked a few hours ago, makes my dick hard. The blood trickles from the artwork as the black seeps into the open abrasion on her lower back.

The emblem of the Sovereign that will forever stain her skin and mine makes me smile. She took all my father had to give, and she fought back. Her fire, her confidence, and that goddamned sassy mouth are what I live for now.

Dahlia walked into this town as a stranger, and she's become so much more. She's family, she's part of the Sovereign, she's a fucking Crown.

"Ouch," Dahlia whimpers, causing me to turn my attention to the artist who I've known most of my young life—Billy. The one man I've come to trust.

Philipe stalks into the room, his gaze set on the scene before him. On Dahlia. I want to punch him. When I woke up and saw his arms around her, I wanted to kill him, but I knew I could trust Philipe.

He glances my way, lifting his hand in greeting. "Brother." Philipe settles beside me to watch my girl get her ink. "I thought you'd have been to the house."

"I don't want to be near that place, at least for a while. Dahlia needs time." The past is far too prominent right now, and I don't know how to get over what happened. I don't want to be a Lancaster, only because of what our father did. But I know it's time for Philipe and me to make things right.

"Does *she* need time, or do *you* need time?"

"When are you going back to New York?" I question, ignoring his question, pinning him with a glare.

A low chuckle vibrates in his chest, and he pats me on the back in a show of camaraderie. After everything that's happened, I think Philipe and I have grown closer. I respect him, I've seen a different side to my brother, one that I hope to get to know better.

"Tomorrow, I'll be out of your hair, and away from Dahlia," he whispers, leaning in. "Do you think she wants me?" He tilts his head to glance over at her as she slips the tank top she's wearing over her slim frame.

"Fuck off, Philipe."

"Just about, I think it's time I let you run the house," he tells me, sitting back as he regards me. "But remember, little brother, I'm not too far away." With a wink, he rises and goes over to Dahlia who's watching us with a shrewd glare.

"Are you two fighting?"

"Debating," Philipe tells her. "I'm leaving tonight. Perhaps you and Ares would like to visit New York sometime?" He winks at her before planting a chaste kiss on her cheek.

"You have to come back, though." Her

voice is filled with hope, and I wonder if she likes having a big brother around.

"I'll be back, sweetheart," he tells her. "Look after him, he's a loose cannon without you around."

"Fuck off, bro," I bite out as I near them. Tarian enters the moment Philipe leaves, and Etienne joins us a moment later with a grin on his face.

"Yo," he greets me, giving me a one-armed hug. "Hey, pretty lady," he coos at my girl, and I'm ready to punch him the fuck out. "Hey hey, I'm just greeting her." He looks at me sheepishly, and I can't help but chuckle at the god of love before me. Jesus, he's so cliché.

"Where to?" Tarian glances between us.

"Party at the Lake House?" I offer, knowing I have two large properties in my grasp, and with my father sitting in prison for the rest of his natural and unnatural life, I plan to make the next few years of my life worth the pain we went through.

Dahlia

THE TABLE WE'RE SEATED AT IS LONG, MADE OF heavy stone, and each seat is filled with the men who have been there for me since the night Abner shot Ares. And I don't know how I would've gotten through it without them.

I glance around taking in Philipe, Ares, Tarian, and Etienne. I don't feel alone in the world anymore. Even though I have my grandmother, she doesn't understand what this society means. It opens doors, it allows those at the table power. Most of the past Crowns abused their power and used it to hurt others.

But we're a new generation.

We will right their wrongs.

"We had a hit on Fergus," Tarian speaks, handing the iPad to Philipe. "He's been seen in Europe. We don't know where the daughter is, and it looks like our connections have gone silent again."

"We'll find her and him," Ares looks at me

as he says this. He knows I'm anxious to learn where my friend could've disappeared to. His hand finds mine, as he offers me a small smile — one that makes my heart do stupid things in my chest.

"Anything else?" Philipe questions. Silence is his response, and he nods. "Good, I'm flying back to New York tonight. I'll put feelers out in Europe; hopefully, someone will get us something we can use."

"I'm flying to London next week," Etienne suddenly bursts out.

All eyes are on him when Philipe asks, "Why?" I know he liked Rukaiya, and I wonder if he's going to see if he can find her. Perhaps he has the connections to do it. Maybe, just maybe, he does know where she is.

"I need to get away from Tynewood for a while. Also, my mother wants to go to some fashion show." He doesn't look at Ares or me, and my senses prickle with awareness. He's hiding something.

"Well, since you're heading to that side of the pond, I have a few things to discuss with you," Ares says suddenly. "How about a drink at the house before everyone goes their separate ways?"

"I don't know."

"Yes, come on, you owe it to me to see if I can handle my beer while you're gone." Ares chuckles when he gets the finger from Etienne as a response.

"Fine. Let's go," he finally acquiesces, and soon, we're in the cars heading to the Lancaster house.

"Do you think maybe Etienne knows where Rukaiya is?" I ask, as we slowly make our way up the long drive moments later.

Ares is quiet, forcing me to glance his way. His focus is on the windshield, but his knuckles are white as he grips the steering wheel.

"What are you not telling me?"

"There are a lot of secrets in this world, little flower," Ares tells me. "And sometimes, it's best that you don't know what the plan is, because, if it goes sideways, you won't be dragged through the mud."

"Ares, for god's sake, you better tell me what the fuck is going on." We come to a stop outside the house; Ares kills the engine and turns his attention on me. Hazel eyes hold me, hostage, piercing me right to the very core.

"Rukaiya's in London, but we're not sure where or why. We're also not sure if she's taken her father's side in this, or if she's being held against her will."

"Why didn't you say anything in there?" I gesture to the place we just left.

"Because it's better to have Etienne go alone. Tarian will follow a few days after, and then, I was planning on surprising you with a beautiful summer European trip to find your best friend."

My mouth falls open in shock, but no words come out. I'm not sure what to say, so I say nothing at all. Ares leans over the center console and presses his lips to mine.

"Don't tell me I never plan surprises because when I do, that stubborn little mouth of yours spoils it."

"What are you going to do about it?" I

arch a brow in question, already knowing the answer.

With a wicked smirk, Ares chuckles. "When we're alone, you'll be very busy swallowing my cock, little flower." He pushes his door open and exits the vehicle. Seconds later, he's beside me, helping me from the car, as we head inside.

"I look forward to the war," I whisper before we're joined by the guys.

"So do I, little flower, so do I."

BONUS SCENE
Etienne

The looming structure of Big Ben shadows me in the dimly lit streets. The corner of the meeting point we set for tonight is where I'm hidden. Since I arrived two days ago, I've been inundated with messages from Dahlia. Ares told her about my contact in the city who had spotted a pretty girl being escorted into a nightclub by two large, burly men.

The photo that I was sent showed the blonde-haired beauty who captured my attention the moment she stepped onto campus, almost a year ago. I watch the crowds of people walking across the bridge, taking in every face I see, praying I notice one person in particular. With every smile and each laugh, I wait to hear her voice, but none of them are

385

her.

It doesn't take long for me to see him nearing me. Isaac saunters up to me carrying a folder, which I'm guessing has all the information I asked for, in his hand.

"Nice to see you this side of the pond," he grins. His British accent is thick when he speaks, and I immediately recognize the scar that runs up his left cheek.

"I've been wanting to visit for a long time," I tell him. "But life gets in the way of having fun." We shake hands before he offers me the folder. I don't know if I want to see what's inside. Are there more secrets we're about to uncover?

Flicking the folder open, I scan the image on the first page. It's definitely her. Rukaiya. But in the photo, her hair is colored a deep red.

"You sure this was the girl?" Isaac questions then. I nod slowly, reading the information about her flying to Germany, Amsterdam, and then Brussels. Two weeks ago, she landed in London, spotted in the West End on the arm of an older man. Flicking the page, I find a photo of them arm in arm, and I don't recognize him.

"Who's the asshole in the expensive suit?"

"That my dear boy is Remington Calvert, you know his nephew," Isaac informs me, causing my gaze to snap to his in shock.

"Tarian's uncle?"

Isaac nods. "Apparently. He's been underground for about fifteen years. The Sovereign kept him safe when he was going to be arrested for running an illegal operation throughout Europe and Asia."

"And, do I want to know what this illegal operation is?" Even as I ask the question, I realize I don't want to know. My best friend, well one of them, has been through everything with me. All three of us grew up together, and ever since we learned about Ares' dad, I hoped the rest of our story will be less dramatic.

I wanted to fly to London, find Rukaiya, and bring her home to America, to Tynewood, where she belongs. But it seems there are far more secrets that have been hidden in the name of the Gilded Sovereign.

"He's the head of a company called Candy

Cane," Isaac informs me. "The information is on page seven. You may want to read it." His voice is low, a whisper of conspiracy heavy in his tone.

I flip to the page in question and bile rises in my throat the moment I read about the company in question. The burning sensation brings tears to my eyes. I don't know how Tarian is going to take this. And I have no idea if he's even going to want to know, but he deserves the truth.

Even if it is hard to hear.

Learning about the dark past of people you call family is a bitter pill to swallow, but Tarian isn't alone. He has us—the Sovereign.

"Thanks for everything, Isaac," I tell my informant. The man who I grew up calling Dad. As much as I know he didn't want to leave us, he had to. My mother forced him to walk away when she learned about the society. Even as the wife of one of the most powerful men in the world, she hated what the Sovereign stood for. She didn't even want me joining, but I'm already inked, sworn in, and now, it's my life.

FIND DANI
Online

Do you follow me?
If not, head over to any of the below sites,
I love to hear from my readers!

Amazon - http://bit.ly/DaniAmazon
BookBub - http://bit.ly/DaniBookBub
Facebook - http://bit.ly/DaniFBPage
Facebook Group - Dani's Deviants
Goodreads - http://bit.ly/DaniGoodreads
Twitter - @danireneauthor
Pinterest - @danireneauthor
Instagram - @danireneauthor
Spotify - http://bit.ly/DaniSpotify

ABOUT THE
Author

Dani is a USA Today Bestselling Author of dark and deviant romance with a seductive edge.

Originally from Cape Town, South Africa, she now lives in the UK with her better half who does all the cooking while she writes all the words. When she's not writing, she can be found binge-watching the latest TV series, or working on graphic design either for herself, or other indie authors. She enjoys reading books about handsome villains and feisty heroines, mostly dark, always seductive, and sometimes depraved. She has a healthy addiction to tattoos, coffee, and ice cream.

www.danirene.com
info@danirene.com

ALSO BY
the author

Deviant (Black Mountain Academy)

Taboo Novellas

Sunshine and the Stalker (collab. with K Webster)

His Temptation

Austin's Christmas Shortcake

Crime and Punishment (Newsletter Exclusive)

Tempting Grayson

Gilded Sovereign Series

Cruel War (Book #1)

Volatile Love (Book #2)

Sins of Seven Series

Kneel (Book #1)

Obey (Book #2)

Indulge (Book #3)

Ruthless (Book #4)

Bound (Book #5)

Envy (Book #6)

Vice (Book #7)

The Taken Series

Stolen

Severed